I0532854

My Faith Was Weaker Than I Thought

52 week Challenge
to Strengthen your Faith
- Use a Compass, Not a Map -
"dies Solis"

by Christian Crafts

COPYRIGHT AND BOOK INFORMATION

The Amazon Endure typeface was designed by 2K/DENMARK in 2025

Published by **ChristianCrafts.us**
Cover Art by **ChristianCrafts.us**
Contact **books@christiancrafts.us**

Copyright © 2026 by ChristianCrafts.us
All rights reserved.

1st Release date: February 2026
Book information: 123pages - 26k, Paperback 5x8in, cream paper
Amazon KDP ASIN: B0GLY272GF

ISBN: 979-8-9947952-0-0

Visit Christian Crafts website:

https://books.christiancrafts.us

A honest feedback about this book is very appreciated.
Please visit my website and join the international book reading
and bible study community.
Thank you.

May God bless you all, yours Christian Crafts

☞ This book is intentionally printed in small pocket book format.
Why you may ask - the reason is simple. So you can have this book with
you all day, at work - beside your bed - in the glove box of your car -
you name it .. and it's always ready for you to read and work with.
Additional you can use the notes section for your own inspiration.

DEDICATION

This book is a quiet space, a place for all hearts, regardless of belief, path, or name.

It was never meant to own the road, but to walk beside you, where the road leads you.

Within its pages, there is woven silence, like a thread stitching together it whispers of those who seek, the musings of the still, and the prayers of the restless.

For this book is not only for those who call out to a god - it's for anyone who calls out, and no answer is unwelcome here.

May its pages hold not just words, but breath, time, and the courage to pause before the quietest questions and the loudest storms.

May you find here not just a form to fill, but an invitation: to listen, to wonder, and to be held, even in the unanswered.

And if the words aren't always smooth that's okay. They can be tender. Angry. Confused. Like prayer often is - real.

So open it when the nights are heavy, when the road seems endless, when you're uncertain of the way forward, or when you're certain, only to need it later.

For every name, every name you choose not to give, every faith or fragment of it, this book is yours.

With a place for all.

So that said - this book is dedicated from you for you.

ABOUT THIS BOOK

WHY CHRISTIAN PRAYER'S STRUCTURE FEELS LIKE COMING HOME

Prayer isn't some rigid, boxed-in exercise - it's a conversation shaped by love, raw honesty, and the slow humbling of our hearts before the God who already knows *everything*. But there's a reason believers have been wrapping their requests, confessions, and gratitude into a certain rhythm for centuries. It's not just theology; it's *theology with skin on*.

1. THE GOD WE MEET IN CONFESSION

Confession isn't about reciting sins like a checklist - though sometimes that's exactly where it starts. It's the place where holiness (that overwhelming sense of God's perfection) slams into our brokenness like a door to an ice cream shop slamming into a brick wall. Think of Isaiah's moment when he said, *"Woe is me!"* - not because God scolded him, but because *God spoke*. Confession doesn't shrink God down to fit our mess. It does the opposite: it makes our mess *smaller* in the presence of the One who judges but *chooses* to forgive.
That's the tension. It's like sitting in a judge's courtroom - except the judge isn't there to sentence you; they're there to take your case personally and *declare you innocent*. Jesus says as much: *"Forgive .. if you forgive others"*. Confession isn't just about wiping the slate clean - it's realizing that the slate was never about *us*. It was about *His* perfect law and His love for us anyway.

2. THANKSGIVING: GRATITUDE AS A SPIRITUAL WORKOUT

Praise doesn't sound like *"Wow, God, that was really good!"* - it sounds like a man whose hand was paralyzed clapping madly because it *moved*. Thanksgiving is that gasp of a soul whose only currency is gratitude, but whose debt is infinite. It's Psalm in the voice of someone who's just had their hand *fully* restored - the kind of praise that sounds like, *"How did I walk around blind for years and not see what was right here in front of me?"*
Here's the beauty: it's not just about listing God's blessings like a laundry list. It's *tasting* them. Like a refugee who's been given more than they imagined, or a parent in debt who gets a check for more than their whole year's worth - gratitude isn't just thanks. It's *shaking the pen from God's hand and staring at the number in disbelief*.
Philipians says to *"be anxious for nothing"* because *"your .. needs will be made known to God."* Thanksgiving is the flip side of that coin: a prayer where you say, *"God, I see what you've already done. Show me where my not-seeing is hurting my heart."*

3. PETITION: BRINGING NEEDS TO THE GOD WHO ALREADY KNEW THEM

Petition isn't about *"fix me"* - though that's often what gets whispered. It's about surrendering your questions like a child pointing at a rainbow and yelling, *"That's NOT a road to Kansas!"* - because sometimes we pray to a God who's already on the road with us.

"Give us this day our daily bread" doesn't mean *"Drop food on my door-step, God, ASAP."* It means *"Here are the breadcrumbs; walk with me, I'm afraid to ask."* Petition is when you admit, *"I don't have all the answers - but I trust You to know when 'no' is kinder than 'yes'."* It's like when your friend calls you in the middle of a storm and you don't rush to fix it. You just *listen* with a hand on the phone. Petition is the *"Please listen; my hands are shaking"* of prayer.

WHY THIS RHYTHM KEEPS US REAL

This isn't a theological blueprint. It's a *way of life* - wounded, loved, and learning to see God differently.

1. FROM BROKEN TO BELOVED

Confession is the place we remember *why* God even speaks: because *we* made a mess of things first. Thanksgiving is where we realize *He* was already on His way to save us.

2. FROM SCARCITY TO GRATITUDE

We're always tempted to pray from lack. *"Give me this, give me that, and here's my checklist."*
But thanksgiving flips that: *"You've already given me this - what do I need to see it more?"*

3. FROM CONTROL TO TRUST

Petition is where we pray not just to get answers but to *pray into answers* - to watch God write His wisdom into our lives instead of us shouting directions at Him.

THE WHY OF THE WHOLE THING

This structure isn't about box checks. It's about *experiencing* what it means to sit beneath God like a child beneath a parent who *might* not answer how we want - but won't ever not answer.
Confession = *"I'm small. You're big. Keep being big."*
Thanksgiving = *"Your goodness is huge - this isn't the end of the story."*
Petition = *"If Your will is not my will, fine - teach me to kneel for both."*

FINAL THOUGHT:

Imagine praying like a teenager talking to a dad who's already in the room: sometimes you apologize, sometimes you say thank you, sometimes you ask for guidance - but the whole time you're sensing the warmth of love around you. *That's* the rhythm of prayer. Not because God needs to hear it; because we need to *believe* it's being heard.

So let's get started .. pick a random week,
get inspired by a topic of the table of contents
or go direct to the current week of the liturgical calendar.

Get **inspired**,
reflect,
and have a bible ready,
to **deepen your understanding in the Holy Scriptures**.

Your travelling companion Christian Crafts

CONTENTS

WEEK 1 - THE DAWN OF HOPE: PREPARING FOR THE RETURN OF LIGHT

SHORT PRAYER

Lord, keep me awake to Your call - not out of fear, but out
of love for the Light that is coming. May I prepare my
heart, discard the weight of this age, and stand firm in Your
peace. Help me see You in all things, that my life may reflect Your kingdom here on earth. Amen.

LONG PRAYER

Oh, Heavenly Father,

Your Word calls us to watchfulness, but not the hollow
kind that binds or burdens. In Isaiah, we glimpse Your rule
over nations, where swords become plowshares and all
people walk in righteousness. Romans reminds us that the
night is almost over; Christ's return is at hand, and our call
is to step out of darkness into Your morning. But first, we
must rid ourselves of unrighteousness, for what dethrones
Christ in our lives?

CONFESSION:

Lord, I confess my neglect. I let busyness dull my spirit, and my own
judgments distract me from the One who alone judges fairly. Forgive me
for storing up earthly treasures instead of seeking Your kingdom. I've ignored the warnings - perhaps treating Your return as a distant myth
rather than the fire that will one day purify the world. Purify my hands
and my heart, O God, that I might be found holy when You call me. Teach
me to live now as those who await the bridegroom's return. Amen.

THANKSGIVING:

I thank You, Lord, that Your justice is already in motion - sovereign over
nations and yet patient with us. Your peace is not the absence of struggle, but the assurance that even in chaos, Your love endures. I praise You

for turning strangers into brothers under Your banner. Let the fruits of Your Spirit - joy, patience, kindness - root themselves deeper in my soul, so that the world sees no shadow of fear, but only the light of Your redemption. Amen.

PETITION:

Teach me, Father, to watch without weary eyes, to walk in Your truth without stumbling, and to love with Your boldness. Give me the courage to let go of what cannot last - to stop clutching at my own agendas and to instead hold fast to Your promises. Let my life be a vessel of peace, a testament to Your mercy, until the day Your kingdom shines in full glory. Watch over Your Church, Lord, that we might stand unshaken as You reveal Your glory. Amen.

Summary:

This week's verses call us into a posture of watchful hope, bridging the tension between the "already" of Christ's kingdom and the "not yet" of its fullness. Isaiah's vision of nations bowing before God contrasts with Matthew's warning about suddenness - we are to live as if the world is ending, but always with the conviction that Christ's peace is here. Romans urges repentance not as shame, but as realignment with the divine order. The heart of this week's prayer is to let go of earthly distractions and embrace a life ready for Your return.

Bible Reference: Isaiah 2:1-5 / Romans 13:11-14 / Matthew 24:37-44

My own inspiration, thoughts and notes:

WEEK 2 - ROOTS OF HOLINESS: DIVINE RESTORATION AND UNITY

SHORT PRAYER

> **Lord, root me in Your Spirit like a shoot from Your stump - let Your hope spring up anew in me. Break the hardness of my heart that I may taste the sweetness of Your grace afresh. May my life flourish in Your righteousness. Amen.**

LONG PRAYER

> **Abba, You sent Your Spirit, O God, not to leave us as orphans, but to water the roots of Your kingdom within us. In Isaiah, the broken branches are renewed; the Messiah, Your son from Jesse's line, will restore the earth and bind hearts together. Paul speaks of hope that does not disappoint - that through our struggles, love matures within us. But Lord, where does my hope lie? In success? In control? Or in the small, tender roots of Your love growing deep?**

CONFESSION:

Have mercy, Lord. I've allowed my faith to become a matter of performance rather than communion - preaching with my mouth but forgetting to love from my soul. Forgive me for my division over petty things, for my harsh judgments that divide rather than bind. I've trusted in my own strength to endure, instead of leaning on Your promise that You will never break Your covenant. Make my heart flexible, like the shoot in Your verse, that it might bear fruit for Your glory alone. Amen.

THANKSGIVING:

I give You thanks for the messiah who makes straight what I make crooked - healing my brokenness with His holiness. Thank You for the Spirit that transforms weakness into strength, doubt into hope. Every fracture within me You knit together with Your hands. Let me rejoice in Your grace that outdoes my sin, like a seed that rises after the cold ground turns warm. Amen.

PETITION:

Lord, let me become one of those who wait - not for comfort in the ways of the world, but for Your presence to break through. Teach me to trust You in my wounds, to rely on Your strength in my weakness. Bind my heart to Your people, that we may be known by the world for Your love that heals and reconciles. Give me courage to walk out my calling: not as a lone branch, but as a shoot in the wild garden of Your Church. Amen.

Summary:

These verses tell a story of restoration. Isaiah's stump of Jesse and the new shoot (Christ) promise a time when the earth's wounds - both natural and spiritual - are healed. Paul reminds us that suffering has a purpose: it builds endurance, character, and hope in our collective pilgrimage. John the Baptist's message of repentance echoes Isaiah: the world is ripe for change, and God's mercy is already at work. This week's prayer is about embracing God's restoration - not in grand gestures, but in the quiet, day-by-day surrender of His Spirit into every root of our lives.

Bible Reference: Isaiah 11:1-10 / Romans 15:4-9 / Matthew 3:1-12

My own inspiration, thoughts and notes:

WEEK 3 - THE WAY OF THE COMFORTED: HOPE IN WEARINESS

SHORT PRAYER

Father, lift the weight from my shoulders like dust before a wind. Make my weary spirit rise on wings of Your promise. Show me the path of life, Lord, even when the road is hard. Amen.

LONG PRAYER

Lord, Sovereign of Life,

You speak of dryness becoming bloom, and stammering lips becoming song - yet You also reveal a John who question Your purpose. The world is a desert; faith is often exhausted. But You, O God, say, "Be strong and hold on! Your salvation is near!" (James). Show me how to bear my weariness for others, as You've bore it for me.

CONFESSION:

Forgive me, Lord, for my impatience with the slow hand of Your healing. I've judged my brokenness more harshly than You do - I've prayed for dry streams to be filled but ignored my own cracked heart. Have mercy on my hardness toward myself and others. Forgive me for doubting Your promise, for mistaking waiting as neglect. You are still here, even in the desert; Your mercy never ends. Amen.

THANKSGIVING:

I praise You, O God, for the times You've given water to my thirsty soul: the unexpected strength, the laughter through tears, the peace that passes understanding. Every miracle of grace is Your signature, written in my bones. Let Your salvation be the daily bread of my soul, and the strength for my hands that have failed. Amen.

PETITION:

Teach me, Lord, to live like a people who have seen Your healing. Help me notice others stumbling in the dust, and reach out as Christ reached for me. Plant your hope deep in my spirit, that when I stumble, my feet may be anchored in Your faithfulness. Let my hope not be empty but full of the life You offer - here, now, and forever. Amen.

Summary:

This week's scriptures are a call to lament and live in hope. The wilderness opens into blooming fields where the weak are upheld, while James and John both wrestle with doubt: one in frustration, one in disbelief. The heart of the matter? Hope does not require answers yet. It means trusting God even when the path is unclear. This prayer is a prayer of holding on - to the divine promise that God's comfort turns our deserts into springs.

Bible Reference: Isaiah 35:1-6a, 10 / James 5:7-10 / Matthew 11:2-11

My own inspiration, thoughts and notes:

WEEK 4 - BRIDAL LIGHT: THE INCARNATION'S PROMISE

SHORT PRAYER

Holy God, I worship the Child Who humbled Himself to walk among us. Fill my heart with awe, and let my life reflect the light of Your incarnate presence. Amen.

LONG PRAYER

Father of Light, You revealed Yourself in a manger to a world enthralled by darkness - yet how fragile, how ordinary, Your first revelation seems! Isaiah foretold it all: a virgin carrying hope, Your son Immanuel, a sign You will protect. Your love is not grand speeches but tender obedience: a baby, an exile, a life laid low for us. Lord, I bow my heart. In this season of shadows, how do I honor the light You bring? Do I make Your gift into a thing, a story, or a god? Or do I kneel like Mary, and say, Behold?

CONFESSION:

Forgive me, Lord, for the ways I've missed Your humility. How many times have I traded Your gifts for more? For greater titles, deeper pockets, more control? I confess my idolatry - be it success, or even "godly busyness" - anything that keeps me from bowing to the manger. Help me see how even my worship can be a sacrifice that honors my pride instead of You. Amen.

THANKSGIVING:

Thank You, Father, that Your love did not wait for my holiness - it came to me in weakness. Jesus is God among us, but He did not come as the king I deserved, or the hero I imagined. He came to Mary, a carpenter's child, and to a stable. Let the awe of Your gift wash over my soul, that no man-made altar can replace. Let me taste Your glory in the ordinary. Amen.

PETITION:

Fill me with the holy fear and humility of Your birth, Lord. Teach me to trust Your way - the way of poverty, service, and love - for it is the only path to life. Grant me eyes to see Your presence hidden in the lives of the young, the rejected, the least of all. Let my faith be as the dawn: small yet powerful, full of promise. Amen.

Summary:

These verses remind us that God does not wait for our readiness; He comes to us in human form, in the most ordinary ways. Isaiah's prophecy is not a future hope but a reality - a baby born, a sign, a light that cannot be snuffed. Matthew's Gospel shows obedience in action: a child born, an angel protecting, a family leaving and returning to fulfill God's purpose. This week's prayer is a response of awe and reverent surrender to the mystery of the Incarnation - and to its ongoing work in hearts who bend before It.

Bible Reference: Isaiah 7:10-14 / Romans 1:1-7 / Matthew 1:18-24

My own inspiration, thoughts and notes:

WEEK 5 - HONORING THE SACRIFICE: TRUST, OBEDIENCE AND HOPE IN EXILE

SHORT PRAYER

Father, help me walk by faith when my way is obscure, to surrender my plans to Yours, and to praise You for the sacrifices that bear Your glory. Amen.

LONG PRAYER

Loving God, Father of all,
What does it mean to surrender a child, a life, to Your purposes? Joseph, weeping with the world's rejection, follows Your call by fleeing, by sacrificing. Wisdom says fear God, honor your father, but life often pulls at our hearts: our wills, our fears, our dreams. Yet in every exile, in every silent step, You are already moving. Would You trust a child? Would You obey a parent who did not understand, yet said, "Go"?

CONFESSION:

Lord, I confess my selfishness - my fear that obedience will cost me. How often I've treated Your commands as options, not anchors. I ask for grace to release my grip on control. Forgive me for the ways I've tested You, my prayers, my patience. You gave the world not a king in a palace, but a child in exile. Will I dare follow where You lead, or cling to my own plans? Amen.

THANKSGIVING:

Thank You, Father, for the moments when my will bowed, and You carried me. I praise Your hand in the chaos: the open doors, the unexpected peace. You made a way in the wilderness - how did I miss it? Let me be as the child, ready to obey, trusting even when I do not understand. Amen.

PETITION:

Teach me to say "Yes" when my instincts say "No." Guard me from pride, from self-reliance. May I, like Joseph, trust You with my life - not as a transaction, but as worship. Protect those I love in my care. Let my steps be gentle, like a tender child; my faith, as unshaken as Your love. Amen.

Summary:

These passages weave trust into obedience. God's command to Ahikar to train his son in the way he should go echoes the sacredness of life and purpose - yet it was in exile that a child's life was protected and a nation's hope was restored. The Wisdom of Jesus' father shows love is not indulgence but devotion. This week's prayer is a prayer of letting go - of control, of fear, of our own wisdom - to trust in God's unfolding plan even when it seems cruel.

Bible Reference: Sirach 3:2-6, 12-14 / Colossians 3:12-21 (or 3:12-17) / Matthew 2:13-15, 19-23

My own inspiration, thoughts and notes:

WEEK 6 - THE LIGHT OF GOD'S GLORY IN DARKNESS

SHORT PRAYER

Lord, as the darkness fades, let your glory break through our shadows. May we, like the Magi, seek you with open hearts and offer our gifts of faith. Stir in us the hunger to follow your light into a new dawn. Amen.

LONG PRAYER

Lord, you have declared, "The darkness shall cover the earth, but you, O Lord, will shine upon us". In a world still veiled by fear and distraction, I long for your radiance to pierce the deep night of my own heart.

CONFESSION:

Sometimes, Lord, I let busyness and fear cloud my eyes - like the Magi's journey was delayed by their own indecision. Forgive me for letting petty doubts slow my worship, for turning back when I should have pressed on. Teach me to discard all excuses and cast them at your feet, as the wise men laid down every pride to find you. Amen.

THANKSGIVING:

You are the dawn of justice, King of kings. Thank you for sending your light first to the smallest, the lost, the hungry. Even now, you illuminate my path with gifts I didn't ask for: grace when I faltered, perspective when I was blind, and a home beyond my wildest dreams when I was adrift. Let me become a vessel for your mercy, just as you turned strangers into a pilgrimage of wonder. Amen.

PETITION:

Lord, as the Magi knelt before a child - humble, unexpected, good enough - remind me that my "worship" doesn't have to be perfect. Give me a heart eager to kneel, whether in sacred places or the dust of daily life. When I'm tempted to hoard my devotion for "earned" moments, show me the child in the corner, waiting for my scattered gifts of praise. Make my yes to you louder than my excuses. Amen.

Summary:

This week's readings illuminate God's radical inversion: the world's "darkness" becomes his theater of glory, while Paul marvels at how the church is a bridge for Gentiles to meet his light. The Magi's story reminds us God meets us - not in perfection, but in our humility, as we offer what we have, not what we claim to deserve.

Bible references: Isaiah 60:1-6 / Ephesians 3:2-3a,5-6 / Matthew 2:1-12

My own inspiration, thoughts and notes:

WEEK 7 - THE SERVANT'S LIGHT IN A BROKEN WORLD

SHORT PRAYER

Lord, you called me to be a servant - gentle, strong, and unyielding in your truth. Let me step into the wilderness of obedience today, trusting you'll be my anointing. Fill me with your Spirit, so the world sees your fire in my hands.

Amen.

LONG PRAYER

Lord, Isaiah's servant sings of a man who does not cry out or lift up his voice - yet the world groans because you've made him their light. How quiet my faith becomes when I mistake my silence for safety. Help me trust that even my whispers carry weight in your hands.

CONFESSION:

I pretend I'm stronger than the servant who needed healing before he could heal. I measure my worth by what I do, not by how you've set me free. Forgive me, Lord, for the times I've let my pride drown out my cries for mercy. Teach me to kneel before my work as John knelt before you - not to earn my call, but to receive it. Amen.

THANKSGIVING:

You sent John the Baptist to prep the way, a man of fire and resolve. Thank you for making his wilderness my classroom: here, I learned that wild obedience is not rebellion, but surrender. Thank you for the disciples who dropped nets and followed - not because they had it all figured out, but because they saw you. When I stumble, may I rest in your promise: "I am with you". Amen.

PETITION:

Lord, like the servant, make me blind to my own plans. Give me eyes to see only your face in the crowd, hearts to serve without counting the cost. Even now, anoint my hands to heal what breaks my own bones, my tongue to name the lies that grip this world. Let no one say they didn't see the light because I failed to hold it. Amen.

Summary:

Isaiah's servant is both fragile and fearless: he bends but doesn't break, whispers but isn't silenced. Acts and John's baptism show how God's people - flawed, hungry, and human - are chosen as his voice and hands. The theme: light isn't about being "perfect"; it's about letting God's fire work through our cracks.

Bible references: Isaiah 42:1-4,6-7 / Acts 10:34-38 / Matthew 3:13-17

My own inspiration, thoughts and notes:

WEEK 8 - THE ANOINTED ONE AND THE BROKEN CHURCH

SHORT PRAYER

Lord, you called me by name while I was still broken. Fill my cracks with your Spirit so the world sees not my mess, but your mercy. Make me a name to be spoken over others. Amen.

LONG PRAYER

Lord, Isaiah's servant is already shaped in darkness, yet you say: "I was exulting over you." How can you love a vessel you first made - one you know will fail and bleed? Yet you call me anyway.

CONFESSION:

I hide behind my "calling" like a shield, Lord. When Paul writes to "the called in Christ Jesus", I'd rather cling to my achievements than my stains. Forgive me for pretending I'm not also the one who scattered at dawn. Teach me that being "called" doesn't mean being beyond breaking - it means being found amid it. Amen.

THANKSGIVING:

Thank you, Lord, for John's voice crying, "Behold, the Lamb of God!". Even my doubt has a purpose when it leads me to you. Thank you for the church: messy, divided, yet the body where you dwell. Here, no one is perfect enough for you - not yet - but here, you're building something far greater than my hands. Amen.

PETITION:

Lord, take my brokenness and turn it into a pulpit. When I'm tempted to whisper my unworthiness, remind me: you named me before the world did. Let my "foolishness" become your wisdom. Give me a heart to see in others what you see in me - a work in progress, but already yours. Amen.

Summary:

Isaiah's servant is both the formed and the shattered - God's chosen and the rejected. The church mirrors this: called, yet splintered, yet held together by the one who made it holy. John's testimony shows how even the "last" man (John) is part of God's "first and last." The theme: holiness isn't escape from brokenness; it's letting God's light redefine what it means to be "called."

Bible references: Isaiah 49:3,5-6 / 1 Corinthians 1:1-3 / John 1:29-34

My own inspiration, thoughts and notes:

WEEK 9 - THE DAWN OF MERCY BREAKS THROUGH

SHORT PRAYER

Lord, thank you for the light breaking through the darkest valleys. Teach me to step into the dawn - not with my strength, but your promise. Make my hands pick up your nets, even when I'm afraid. Amen.

LONG PRAYER

Lord, the prophet sees "but a remnant will return" - and yet, somehow, you've given birth to a son. In that gap between exile and resurrection, you stitch together what the world calls impossible: a child, a light, a people who aren't lost but looked for.

CONFESSION:

I cling to my "rightness" like the Corinthians clinging to party. Lord, forgive me for asking: "Am I called to this? Or was I meant for that?" You've called me to you, but I've traded your mercy for my credentials. Forgive me for waiting for signs like Jesus waited in the wilderness - forgiveness before I'd asked for it. Amen.

THANKSGIVING:

Thank you for saying "no more" to fear. Your yoke is light; your burden is joy. Even when Peter and Andrew abandoned their nets, they heard your voice saying "Follow me". Thank you for turning my confusion into calling, my weakness into witness. Amen.

PETITION:

Lord, like Jesus, I'm driven not by spectacle but by mercy. Send me into the streets - not with a preacher's voice, but with hands ready to mend, ears ready to listen. Let my "small boat" become your fishing net, catching not fish, but souls desperate for your voice. Amen.

Summary:

Isaiah's prophecy and Jesus' early ministry intersect on a single note: God doesn't wait for perfection; he meets us in the dawn. Paul's warning about divisions cuts to the heart: when we start arguing over who's right, we forget the one who's forgiven us. The theme: the kingdom comes not to those who're "prepared," but to those who're willing to step into the light.

Bible references: Isaiah 8:23 - 9:3 / 1 Corinthians 1:10-13,17 / Matthew 4:12-23 (or 4:12-17)

My own inspiration, thoughts and notes:

WEEK 10 - THE SALT OF THE EARTH: HUMBLE AND UNYIELDING

SHORT PRAYER

Lord, you call the poor, the broken, the "foolish" to make you known. May I be your salt - a seasoning that softens hearts and preserves hope. Fill me with your humility and strength. Amen.

LONG PRAYER

Lord, Zephaniah's future promises "the meek will inherit the land". In a world that measures worth by power, you flip the script: the "weak" are your inheritance.

CONFESSION:

I've traded your humility for the world's approval, Lord. Like the Corinthians, I've judged others' "spiritual gifts" while ignoring your cross. Forgive me for mistaking achievement for your blessing. Teach me that my value isn't in what I accomplish, but in what you accomplished for me. Amen.

THANKSGIVING:

Thank you for calling the "foolish" - men and women the world calls nothing - to found your church. Thank you for the Beatitudes, where the mourners and meek inherit a kingdom, not because they're "better," but because they're broken open. When I'm tempted to harden my heart, remind me: your mercy is my strength. Amen.

PETITION:

Lord, make me your salt that "does not lose its flavor". Let my life be a living rebuke to the "strong" who think they've arrived. Give me eyes to see the lonely, the scorned, the "last" - and hands to heal them as you healed me. Even in my weaknesses, let my humility be a weapon, and my mercy a battle cry. Amen.

Summary:

Zephaniah's hope and Jesus' Sermon on the Mount shatter the world's hierarchy: the poor become heirs, the persecuted are your children. Paul's letter exposes the contradiction: God's power isn't in our strength, but in our surrender. The theme: true salt isn't domination; it's a radical surrender that transforms even the earth.

Bible references: Zephaniah 2:3; 3:12-13 / 1 Corinthians 1:26-31 / Matthew 5:1-12a

My own inspiration, thoughts and notes:

WEEK 11 - THE LIGHT WITHIN: LIVING AS WITNESSES TO THE TRUTH

SHORT PRAYER

God of boundless truth, open my eyes to see Your light in every act of kindness and honesty. May I, like salt and light, reflect Your goodness, turning hearts toward Your mercy. Help me walk boldly, fearless of what they call me, for my purpose is to honor You. Amen.

LONG PRAYER

Heavenly Father,

I come before You today, weary but hopeful. My words stumble often - full of fear, hesitation, or distraction - but You call me to clarity, to bear Your light like salt on wounds. Forgive the moments I kept silent when speaking up would have shown Your grace. Purify my speech and actions so they are seasoned with Your truth.

CONFESSION:

O God, I confess my weaknesses. Too often I hide behind excuses when I should act with truth. My fear of judgment makes me passive in Your name, as if my voice holds no weight. Forgive me for prioritizing comfort over Your call. Help me cast aside shame like a heavy cloak, stepping into Your strength. Amen.

THANKSGIVING:

Lord, thank You for revealing Your light within me. You teach me that holiness isn't about being untouched by the world but untaken by it. When I follow Your Word, my life becomes a fragrance of Christ, calling others toward freedom. Thank You for making me salt to preserve others, light to guide their steps. Let me reflect You not in perfection, but in devotion. Amen.

PETITION:

Father, shape my words and deeds into Your truth. When I fear how others will perceive me, let me remember Your glory outshines my flaws. Give me the humility to confess when wrong, the boldness to love without fear, and the endurance to keep shining - even in darkness. Amen.

Summary:

Isaiah speaks of true fasting as releasing the oppressed and feeding the hungry, echoing Paul's message in that His Word must be rooted in faith, not human wisdom. Jesus declares we are salt and light - not to demand attention, but to draw others into His light through our lives.

Bible references: Isaiah 58:7-10 / 1 Corinthians 2:1-5 / Matthew 5:13-16

My own inspiration, thoughts and notes:

WEEK 12 - LOVE REWRITTEN: HEARTS CHANGED BY GRACE'S PEN

SHORT PRAYER

Lord, rewrite my heart with Your love - the kind that bears all things, forgives even its greatest wounds. May my eyes see mercy; my hands reach out; my words speak only life. Let justice and kindness rule where I walk. Amen.

LONG PRAYER

Loving God,

I stand at the foot of Your mercy today, a writer of my own wrongs, a breaker of commandments I barely understood. Your law wasn't meant to crush but to show me how Your love already broke the chains I couldn't undo. I am both the sinner and the saved - not because I earned it, but because You took my rebellious heart and rewrote it in Your image.

CONFESSION:

Lord, I am the lawbreaker - and the broken. I justified my anger as "justified," my jealousy as "righteous," my quick tongue as "honest." Forgive my refusal to see the pain I caused, my blindness to Your image in others. You didn't give commands to damn me; You gave them to redeem me. Amen.

THANKSGIVING:

Lord, thank You for the Cross - where Your perfect love unshackled the imperfect. My righteousness is rags; Your mercy is fire that melts and reshapes. You didn't just overlook my sins, You turned them into steps toward Your justice. Your law isn't a list of dos and don'ts; it's the fingerprint of Your grace written on my soul. Amen.

PETITION:

Father, burn away my pride and replace it with Your love. Let my hands reach for wounds rather than weapons; let my tongue bless rather than wound. Teach me to see You in the angry, the alienated, the abandoned. Turn my heart into Your workshop where Your love takes form. Amen.

Summary:

Sirach warns that without obedience, wisdom can't take root - but in Corinthians, Paul contrasts God's wisdom with human wisdom: it's not about power or eloquence, but the power of the Holy Spirit to transform lives. Jesus then reframes the Law, not to abolish it but to show its heart. Love isn't legalistic; it's revolutionary.

Bible references: Sir 15:15-20 / 1 Corinthians 2:6-10 / Matthew 5:20-22a, 27-28, 33-34a, 37

My own inspiration, thoughts and notes:

WEEK 13 – FALLEN BUT NOT FORGOTTEN: GRACE IN HUMAN FRAILTY

SHORT PRAYER

Lord, we remember our first disobedience, where fear and deception twisted beauty into loss. Yet You met us in our shame with grace - whispers of mercy in the promise of a Seed. Save us from hiding, and fill us with the wisdom to choose life again today. Amen.

LONG PRAYER

Lord, in the garden where the wind carried the lies like whispers from the serpent's tongue, we stand with You to-day - stung by the memory of our own choices. Our hearts are heavier than the dirt You breathed into us, clinging to shame when Your truth is breath. Forgive us for believing that our sin defines our worth, for forgetting that You chase us even when we flee.

CONFESSION:

Father, we bow before the first failure of Your beloved, where the promise of eating from every tree became a burden of hiding. We've let fear replace faith, doubt replace obedience, and pride replace trust. How often we, like Adam and Eve, turn to the shadows of the garden when You are the Light! Forgive our fear of knowing You fully - of being seen, of being held to account - and cleanse us with Your own humility, which stripped Yourself of glory to rescue us. Amen.

THANKSGIVING:

Yet in this place of confession, Lord, You turned the serpent's curse into a sign of salvation. You met Adam and Eve in their exile with tender mercy, though they sought only to blame. You promised to send a Seed who would crush the serpent's head, a foreshadowing of the One who would sit not in the throne of judgment but on the cross. You don't undo our mess; You bear it, You wash it, and You wear it as a scar of Your love.

PETITION:

Lord, we are still tempted like Jesus was in the wilderness - with distractions, half-truths, and the empty voices of this world. Grant us hunger for Your Word alone, not crumbs of convenience or the fleeting promises of power or control. Teach us to fall on Your mercy, not our own strength. And when we fail, as we will, remind us that Your "well done" is the only mark that matters. Amen.

Summary

This week's Scriptures bear witness to humanity's first rebellion and God's stubborn, loving persistence. The fall reveals our capacity for self-betrayal, yet even then, God names Adam and Eve with love, foreshadowing His mercy through the coming Messiah. Satan's temptation targets trust, but Christ's wilderness victory shows that Your strength is what we lack. Your promise - a Seed who will defeat evil - is both a prophecy and a present invitation: "Come, follow me." The cross is the ultimate "well done," where You take on our shame to end our hiding.

Bible References: Genesis 2:7–9; 3:1–7, Romans 5:12–19 (or 5:12, 17–19), Matthew 4:1–11

My own inspiration, thoughts and notes:

WEEK 14 — ABRAM'S CALL: RISK AND RADICAL TRUST

SHORT PRAYER

> Lord, like Abram, we hesitate when You call us to leave
> what feels safe. Teach us to trust Your promises over our
> plans, and walk - even when the ground is unknown. May
> Your name be our guide, not our fear. Amen.

LONG PRAYER

> Father, this week, we see the boldest step of faith - the
> moment You told Abram, "Go," and he walked away from
> everything familiar. No roadmap, no promise of comfort,
> only Your voice breaking through the noise like a lullaby.
> You ask us the same today: "Will you leave? Will you
> trust?"

CONFESSION:

Lord, we are guilty of loving our idols more than You - our plans, our security, our own wisdom. We stand in Abram's muddy sandals, half-turned to look back, our hearts tied to the known when You whisper of glory ahead. How many times have we said yes to comfort and no to adventure? How often have we bargained with You, offering half-trust and hollow obedience? Amen.

THANKSGIVING:

And yet, even then, You were already writing the stars for Abram. You changed his name from "father of confusion" to "father of many nations," as if to say: "Your name is not yours to keep." You took the childless couple and outnumbered armies, not by their strength, but by Your promise. You didn't promise Abram a life without fear, but a life without empty fear - the kind that forgets You go before. Amen.

PETITION:

Lord, like Abram, we are called to move - not just physically, but inwardly. We cling to control when You call us to surrender. We judge Your timing by our clocks when Your "right now" is eternal. Loosen our grip on the past, steady our feet for the next step, and fill our hearts with the courage of those who believed in the promise of an inheritance we cannot see. Let us, like Your first servant, set our hearts on You instead of our comforts. Amen.

Summary

This week's call is raw with risk - Abram is not a perfect saint, but a man who chooses, over and over, to trust the voice that asks him to walk into the unknown. God's promise is specific: "I will bless you" and "through you, all nations will be blessed." No conditions, no qualifications - just a command and a name change. In Christ, we are the new Abram, called to leave our old lives behind for the land of Your promises, where "I will be your God" isn't a hope, but a present reality.

Bible References: Genesis 12:1–4a, 2 Timothy 1:8b–10, Matthew 17:1–9

My own inspiration, thoughts and notes:

WEEK 15 — LIVING WATER: THIRST AND DIVINE ENCOUNTER

SHORT PRAYER

Jesus, we are thirsty - thirsty for love, for purpose, for You. Like the Samaritan woman at the well, we draw from the wrong places. Quench our hunger with Your living water, that we may give You to others in turn. Amen.

LONG PRAYER

Loving God, this week, we stand at the well with the woman of Samaria, our cups empty, our hearts parched. You, who walked across borders and taboos, meet us in our exhaustion, inviting us to drink from the very source of life. But first, You name us - not our sins, but our deepest longings.

CONFESSION:

Lord, we come like the woman, hands already reaching for another jar of water that won't satisfy. We seek love in fleeting relationships, peace in fleeting achievements, meaning in fleeting moments. We have drawn from the well of others' approval, of our own efforts, of even the lies that promise to fill our hollows. Forgive us for believing that any created thing could hold what only You offer - Yourself. Amen.

THANKSGIVING:

And You, Jesus, showed up at the hottest part of the day, when all else withers. You, the Jew, spoke to the Samaritan, the despised - at a well. You, the King, asked for a drink from a woman the world had written off. You called her "woman," not "girl" or "filthy," but with the weight of her humanity. And then, in that moment, You opened the heavens: "Give me to drink." You did not condemn her thirst; You met it with the promise that "the water [You offer] will become in her a spring of water welling up to eternal life." Amen.

PETITION:

Lord, today, let us not be afraid to approach You with our jars of half-truths and half-hearted lives. Teach us to see Your voice in the whispers of the Spirit, even when the world drowns out Your invitation. Like the Samaritan, may we run with joy to tell others about the One who saw our thirst before we named it. And when we are left empty again, let us remember: "Believe in the One I am sending." Amen.

Summary:

This week's Scriptures reveal God's radical meeting of human need - not with condemnation, but with life. The Samaritan woman's encounter with Jesus strips away every excuse: her past, her people's history, her loneliness. His offer isn't just water; it's a transformation. She runs, not out of shame, but with the news of a Savior who meets her in her most human place. In Christ, You invite us to the same truth: "The Spirit gives life; the flesh profits nothing." Draw from Him, and you will never thirst again.

Bible References: Exodus 17:3–7, Romans 5:1–2, 5–8, John 4:5–42 (or 4:5–15, 19b–26, 39a, 40–42)

My own inspiration, thoughts and notes:

WEEK 16 - THE LIGHT THAT REVEALS: HIDDEN FAITH IN DARKNESS

SHORT PRAYER

O God, when our eyes are blinded by the world's darkness, help us see the truth through Christ. Let Your light shine on our hearts, revealing Your grace where we once saw only doubt. May we trust in Your promises, even when our understanding fails. Amen.

LONG PRAYER

Heavenly Father,

We come before You in faith, just as the blind man did in Your Word - praying not with words of wisdom, but with the cry of a heart that longs to see. Like the shepherds who sought David not in outward appearance but by Your Spirit, show us the truth beneath our own perceptions.

CONFESSION:

Lord, we confess that we too often mistake shadows for light. We have looked for strength in our own plans, like the priests who couldn't bear Jesus' truth. Forgive us when we close our ears to Your voice, when we doubt Your goodness even as You stand before us. Help us humble our hearts, to stop trusting in our own sight and to trust in Your vision for us. Amen.

THANKSGIVING:

Yet Lord, in Your mercy, You have made the way clear even when our vision fails. You turned the darkness of this man's blindness into the light of testimony - how he could not only see, but believe. Thank You that Your ways are higher than ours, and Your choices are always for our good, even when we struggle to see them. In Your Word, You speak a future so certain that even the skeptic stumbles toward it. Amen.

PETITION:

Grant us the same blindness-turned-to-sight, O God. Loosen the bonds of our hesitation so we, too, may testify not just to Your existence, but to Your glory in all things. And as the shepherd anointed David "by the Spirit of the Lord," let Your Spirit choose us from among the people, marking us as vessels of Your light. May every doubt we hold be replaced by Your Word, and every fear by Your promise. Amen.

Summary:

These verses speak to the hidden work of grace: God's choice of David, unseen by mere appearance, contrasts with the miracle of the blind man who knew Jesus as the Son without seeing Him fully. Paul urges us to walk in the light of Christ, while the blind man's testimony reveals the radical nature of faith even in darkness. Together, they call us to trust when our eyes fail, to recognize the Spirit's anointing, and to let God's truth illumine every doubt.

Bible References: 1 Samuel 16:1b, 6-7, 10-13a, Ephesians 5:8-14, John 9:1-41

My own inspiration, thoughts and notes:

WEEK 17 - RAISE THE DEAD WITHIN US: LIFE FROM DESOLATION

SHORT PRAYER

O Lord, when death seems the only answer, remind us You have power over the grave. Raise us from the dust of despair, and let Your life fill every shattered place in us. May we live in the confidence of Your resurrection. Amen.

LONG PRAYER

Heavenly Father,

No cry of the human heart echoes Your Word more than Lazarus' sisters' faith: "If you had been here..." In their sorrow, we recognize the ache of those who have seen life stolen - not just from loved ones, but from dreams, from strength, from hope. Yet You hear them, You answer, and You raise what was lost. Teach us to hope even when our situations look dead.

CONFESSION:

Lord, we fail You in ways that kill our own souls - by turning away from You in bitterness, by giving in to fear, by burying dreams as if You couldn't resurrect them. We stand in the tombs of our failures, thinking our lives are dust, and yet You, Jesus, said to our fears, "I am the resurrection and the life". Forgive us for doubting Your power when the impossible stares us down. Amen.

THANKSGIVING:

Thank You that You enter the darkest caves - caves of depression, addiction, loneliness, and despair - and walk through them with the light of resurrection. You didn't wait for conditions to change; You turned toward the stench of death itself and shouted, "Lazarus, come forth!" Thank You that Your power doesn't depend on our faith alone; it demands nothing but obedience. By Your wounds, we are healed; by Your grave, our own graves become thresholds to new life. Amen.

PETITION:

Now let the Spirit move. Loosen the grave clothes binding us - whether from regret, shame, or resignation. Let Your breath fill our lungs with the newness of life. As You asked Martha to "stop weeping," let us too believe that every "if you had only been here" is met with "I am come that they might have life...". Give us the audacity to believe You work even when all seems lost. Amen.

Summary:

Here, death and resurrection intertwine: Ezekiel's dry bones become the foundation of Israel's hope, just as Paul declares in Christ we no longer walk in our own flesh but in the Spirit. Jesus' cry over Lazarus mirrors the sisters' grief, only His words transform it - from loss to miracle. Together, these passages declare: You are not alone in the valley; Your life is your victory.

Bible References: Ezekiel 37:12-14, Romans 8:8-11, John 11:1-45

My own inspiration, thoughts and notes:

WEEK 18 - THE KING WHO WALKS INTO OUR STREETS: HUMILITY MEETS DIVINITY

SHORT PRAYER

> Lord, the crowds cheered today; the world will betray to-
> morrow. Let me recognize Your glory not just on palms, but
> in my hands and feet. May I walk Your way of love, even
> when it's misunderstood. Amen.

LONG PRAYER

Heavenly Father,

> We come to the paradox of kingship - where power is bent
> into brokenness, and glory appears not in a crown, but in a
> crown of thorns. Your son rides into Jerusalem like a serv-
> ant, not a warrior; and it is in this reversal that the world
> learns true royalty. As we watch Him choose humility over
> entitlement, let His heart become our heart.

CONFESSION:

Lord, we are just as tempted as the soldiers to demand proof of Your authority. We build temples of ambition instead of love, and bow to idols of success rather than You. Forgive us for hiding behind masks of self-reliance, for acting like the rulers who mocked Him, for laughing at the "foolishness" of Your way before we learn its strength. You are the One who "emptied" Himself, yet how often do we fill ourselves instead? Amen.

THANKSGIVING:

Thank You, Lord, that Your most powerful act of love was not in do-minion, but in dying. On that hill, the heavens split, and we learned the power of weakness. The people threw down their cloaks - not to crown You, but to prove they understood: You didn't need their applause to be King. And it is in this moment, where all eyes were on Him yet He saw our hearts, that we catch a glimpse of the Father's plan. Amen.

PETITION:

So teach us, Father: to bow as He bowed, to serve as He served, to let the world's judgment roll off like water if we are found clinging to You instead of their approval. Let our hands lay down whatever we cling to, our tongues cease from boasting, and our lives become the temple You need - where Your mercy overflows, unearned, into the world. Come, Lord Jesus, and make Your throne not just a city, but a life. Amen.

Summary:

The kingdom story is here: Jesus, a king of kings, arrives on a donkey's back, not a horse, proving Isaiah's words that "he took up our infirmities". Philippians' hymn of humility redefines power, while Matthew's passion reveals that the Son of Man's kingship will be won in His surrender. Our part? Surrender first, then follow.

Bible References: Matthew 21:1-11 / Isaiah 50:4-7 / Philippians 2:6-11 / Matthew 26:14-27:66 (or 27:11-54)

My own inspiration, thoughts and notes:

WEEK 19 - THE RESURRECTION'S RADICAL REDEMPTION

SHORT PRAYER

Thank you, Lord, for Peter's bold witness - the same man who denied You now proclaims Your resurrection to all nations. Open our eyes to the truth You rose again, that grace overturns our past and writes our future anew. Fill us with Your peace as we meet the Risen One in the breaking bread of today. Amen.

LONG PRAYER

Heavenly Father, our hearts tremble as we stand at the foot of Your empty tomb, where Peter wept but then leapt forward in joyful faith. In those first moments after sunset on Sunday, the disciples fled in fear, hearts bound by loss and doubt - until You met them, calling us by name even through locked doors. Let Your light break into our shadowed corners today, O Lord. Break the chains of our past fears, and remind us: You are not bound by death; You are the Resurrection that conquers shame and sin alike.

CONFESSION:

Lord, we confess our moments of unbelief, those times we hid in silence instead of proclaiming Your name. We too have stumbled when hope seemed lost, like those two disciples grieving on the road to Emmaus. Forgive us when we walked with You without truly seeing. Wash us with the living water of Your mercy, that we may carry the story of Your triumph wherever we go. Amen.

THANKSGIVING:

Praise You, Creator, for turning emptiness into endless promise! By

Your power, even death was overcome, and life was unleashed. Your resurrection transforms everything - our sins become a story of mercy, our failures become a school for repentance. We thank You for the hands that were nailed, now raised in glory; for the tomb He entered, now an invitation to You, our home. Amen.

PETITION:

Father, send us out like Peter - bold in truth, trembling yet unafraid. Let our words echo Yours: "You must turn!". Give us hunger to share this hope, boldness to meet the broken with Your hope, and ears to hear You when You whisper, "Peace to you" in our deepest silences. Break open our hearts until all see the light You've set ablaze in us. Amen.

Summary:

This week's verses weave the truth of Christ's resurrection into daily life: Peter's witness, the disciples' doubting-and-believing journey, and the empty tomb's call to hope. Jesus meets us where doubt lurks, calling us to turn from old ways to new life. The resurrection is both victory over sin and the promise of eternal communion with Him. Here, failure and faith collide - just as love meets grace. The same risen Christ who walked the earth now walks with us today, rewriting our ending.

Bible references: Acts 10:34a, 37-43 / Col 3:1-4 / John 20:1-9 / Matthew 28:1-10 / Luke 24:13-35

My own inspiration, thoughts and notes:

WEEK 20 - THE CHURCH: ROOTS IN LOVE, GATHERED FOR TRANSFORMATION

SHORT PRAYER

Lord, thank You for the church - flawed but beloved, chaotic yet mighty - where love is shown, mercy overflows, and we taste heaven before it's over. Fill our hearts with fire like those first believers as we join You. Amen.

LONG PRAYER

Lord Jesus, we gather again this week to see Your hands at work in this place. In Acts, the church began not as an institution but as a community where strangers became siblings, the marginalized were welcomed, and every person shared from their abundance. Yet even then, You didn't call us perfect; You called us present - present to each other's needs, present with You in the ordinary. Open our eyes to the miracle around us: this table, this fellowship, this broken bread shared in Your name.

CONFESSION:

Lord, we confess when we fail to be the church You intended - when we hoard our gifts, when we judge instead of welcome, or when we forget You knit us together from our worst and best. Like the early disciples, we too were selfish sometimes, forgetting our first love. Forgive us for the moments we acted like the world. Heal our divisions - let our unity be a sign to the world. Amen.

THANKSGIVING:

Thank You for the gifts of this people: their generosity, their hope, their willingness to bear one another's burdens. You meet us here in the simplest acts - songs lifted in praise, hands stretched out in aid, tears shed and comforted, the word proclaimed and hearts softened. How beautiful when fear gives way to "all hearts were one" and shared possessions like a single heart. Make us so hungry for You that the world sees the change only hope can bring. Amen.

PETITION:

Father, teach us to see one another as You do - every face, every story, a gift to hold and honor. Fill us with a love that's fierce for the lost and gentle with the wounded. Let this place pulse with the Holy Spirit's fire: bold witness, bold love, bold hope. Open our eyes to the hurting in this room; let us be the hands and voice You've placed among us. Build Your church in us. Amen.

Summary:

This week, the New Testament lights up with the early church's dynamic: fire, unity, and purpose. Here, God's grace creates a radical community - one where wealth was shared, doubts were answered, and hearts burned with joy. The church is more than a building; it's where the lost are welcomed, the broken are bound up, and Christ is announced together. That same fire is yours to carry: be present, open-handed, and fire-breathing with love. The world needs to see it in you.

Bible references: Acts 2:42-47 / 1 Peter 1:3-9 / John 20:19-31

My own inspiration, thoughts and notes:

WEEK 21 - THE FIRE OF THE HOLY SPIRIT AND HOPE BEYOND DEATH

SHORT PRAYER

Spirit of God, ignite your fire within me this week. Like the disciples on that first Pentecost, let your presence embolden my words and stir my faith. May I walk through life knowing that Christ is risen, breaking every barrier of doubt and death. Amen.

LONG PRAYER

Lord, your Spirit does not come quietly-it arrives in tongues of flame, tearing down walls and opening hearts. Let me, like the apostles, speak boldly where fear once held my tongue. Fill this season with your power so my testimony is a fire that never dims.

CONFESSION:

I confess, Lord, my doubts creep in-small voices whispering that I don't measure up. But you, O Christ, rose beyond grave's reach, and your resurrection is proof I am loved in my frailty. Forgive me for clinging to fear instead of embracing the wild, reckless love that raised you from the dead. Amen.

THANKSGIVING:

I thank you, Father, for the disciples who walked with Jesus through pain yet knew joy in the end. You took bread and broke it into life eternal for them, and for me. Their story reminds me: your grace writes over grief, and light lingers where shadows seem eternal. Amen.

PETITION:

God, let my life proclaim resurrection-may my words be like tongues of fire that build rather than burn bridges. Heal the silences in my soul where guilt or shame linger. Teach me to speak as one who has already seen the grave undone by your hands. Pour out your Spirit on me so I

might love like Jesus loved: freely, wholeheartedly, beyond my limits.
Amen.

Summary:

This week's verses paint a picture of the Holy Spirit descending in dramatic fashion, breaking chains, and filling believers with an impossible hope. Acts echoes God's presence overwhelming the world, while Peter anchors this glory in Christ's work-his resurrection is the foundation for our faith. Luke's story of the road to Emmaus shows how faith dawns when hearts learn to recognize the risen Christ in ordinary moments.

Bible References: Acts 2:14, 22-33, 1 Peter 1:17-21, Luke 24:13-35

My own inspiration, thoughts and notes:

WEEK 22 - THE BREAD THAT LEADS US HOME

Christ, open my eyes to the Christ in my brooding thoughts and my restless nights. Like the disciples on the road to Emmaus, show me that in the ordinary, you are made present. May I seek you in every broken step, and find your love in my hunger. Amen.

LONG PRAYER

Lord, you walked beside those disciples in disbelief, yet never left them. Even when their hearts were hard as stone, you walked with them, turned their grief into joy. Let me pause often enough to look into your face, as they finally did, and know that you are always close-even when I am blind.

CONFESSION:

I confess I miss you in the mundane: the rush of to-do lists, the noise of the world. Like the disciples, I sometimes pass you on the road without knowing. Forgive my distracted gaze and teach me to stop, to reach out, to taste the broken bread that is your presence among us. Amen.

THANKSGIVING:

I thank you for the disciples who followed you long after all signs of miracle had faded. Your grace shone in their struggle-how you fed them, listened to their doubts, and made themselves your altar. Their story is mine: every heart, every sorrow, every meal is sacrament. Amen.

PETITION:

Jesus, walk with me daily, not in miracles alone but in ordinary kindnesses. Break open the bread of scripture, conversation, and service-may I find you in every act of grace. When I feel lost or small, help me to hear your voice over the din of fear: "Stay with me," for you never abandon me. Amen.

Summary:

This week's texts speak of divine encounters rooted in familiarity-where the ordinary becomes extraordinary, and faith dawns in unexpected moments. Acts recounts the Church's birth with raw conviction, while 1 Peter urges believers to live like the righteous Christ endured. John's metaphor of shepherding and life's abundant doorway anchors hope beyond human frailty.

Bible References: Acts 2:14a, 36-41, 1 Peter 2:20b-25, John 10:1-10

My own inspiration, thoughts and notes:

WEEK 23 - FAITH IN DIVINE UNITY AND PRESENCE

SHORT PRAYER

Lord, as the early church grew in trust and mission, help us
walk in Your unity, open to Your gifts. Fill us with boldness,
knowing You dwell within us. Guide our hands and hearts
to serve with courage and love. Amen.

LONG PRAYER

Lord, sometimes I feel like the widow who couldn't find a
single faithful leader among us - just another empty plea
echoing in the air. But you've made me a living stone too,
though I'm still chipping away at the edges. Show me how
to build Your temple in a world that doesn't see it yet. And
when I stumble, remind me again: You're the only way, the
only door, the one who doesn't just promise a path but is
the path - even when my feet trip over their own doubts.

CONFESSION:

Lord, we admit the times we doubt Your power, questioning how You
move in lives. We confess moments of fear when division replaces love,
where selfishness stifles the Spirit. Forgive us for forgetting You are the
cornerstone, the living stone that holds all together. Guide our hearts to
humility and unity. Amen.

THANKSGIVING:

We thank You for the apostles' bold faith and the Holy Spirit's outpour-
ing. Thank You for making Yourself known through each act of healing
and preaching-where division cracked, Your love filled the void. You meet
us where we are, not as orphans but as adopted children of light. Let us
be Your light to a hurting world. Amen.

PETITION:

Lord, stir in us the same hunger for Your presence that drove the early
believers. Make us a people who step beyond our fears, trusting in the

Father, resting in the Son's promises, and living by the Spirit's power. Help us extend Your compassion, not just in words, but through action-opening doors for Your grace to reach those who need You most. Amen.

Summary:

This week's passage illustrates how believers overcame obstacles by embracing unity, trusting in the Holy Spirit, and witnessing to Christ's power through unity and service. The Scriptures reveal God's hands actively shaping lives, not just by His word but through His people's devotion. We're called to move forward with unwavering faith, just as the disciples did, knowing Christ's presence makes us more than conquerors.

Bible References: Acts 6:1-7 / 1 Peter 2:4-9 / John 14:1-12

My own inspiration, thoughts and notes:

WEEK 24 - SEEKING GOD IN SORROW AND JOY

SHORT PRAYER:

Holy One, walk through our grief with us. Fill our joy with
gratitude for Your salvation and grace. Send Your Spirit to
mend our wounds and lift up our souls. Amen.

LONG PRAYER

Father, just as Simon the Sorcerer saw Your truth set Philip
free - his heart too heavy, yet Your Spirit unstopped his
way - open mine now. When words feel thin, like Peter's
witnesses before kings, fill me with Your breath, so my
trembling hands might still declare Your name. And like Jesus promised, You're right here - not as a distant guide, but
as the air I breathe. Let me love You like the ones I call
loved, and let my life echo the promise: 'I am in You, and
You in me.

CONFESSION:

Lord, we confess the times when sorrow clouded our faith, dimming
our trust in You. We've held on to bitterness when You called us to hope;
we sought comfort in shadows instead of You. Forgive us for ignoring the
power of Your presence in hardship, and help us turn even our losses into
lessons of Your faithfulness. Amen.

THANKSGIVING:

Thank You for the Ethiopian eunuch's story-a moment of salvation in
sorrow. Thank You for the Samaritan woman who met Jesus in her brokenness and found joy in your Word. You are the giver of living water,
turning thirst into trust. Let us praise You for bringing life to dead places
in our lives. Amen.

PETITION:

Lord, where we feel overwhelmed, soften our hearts to receive Your comfort. Where we rejoice, fill us with a steadfast joy that does not waver. Send Your servants to serve others, mirroring Your own boundless grace. Open our eyes to see Your hand in every chapter, so we may walk boldly in both pain and gladness. Amen.

Summary:

These passages teach us that God's salvation shines through even the darkest moments, transforming sorrow into joy through faith and encounter with Christ. From Philip's testimony to the Samaritan's encounter, Scripture reveals a God who pursues lost souls with grace. We're invited to seek Him earnestly, knowing His presence brings true renewal.

Bible References: Acts 8:5-8, 14-17 / 1 Peter 3:15-18 / John 14:15-21

My own inspiration, thoughts and notes:

WEEK 25 - WITNESSING THE RISEN LORD

SHORT PRAYER

Lord, as we remember Your ascension, fill us with purpose and joy in Your mission. Open our eyes to see Your glory in everyday things. Send us forth as witnesses of Your resurrection power. Amen.

LONG PRAYER

Lord, as the apostles waited in that upper room, confused but trusting - just like those first followers - my heart stumbles. You're the same Christ who stood there with wounds yet wonder in His hands, telling us to go, even when the way feels hazy. Help my faith catch fire like the fire of Pentecost, so I won't just hear Your call but follow it like Your name is tied to my breath.

CONFESSION:

Lord, we confess we sometimes forget Your resurrection power in our daily lives. We've treated Your ascension as distant instead of personal- filling our hands with worries instead of sharing Your peace. Forgive us for growing complacent with Your presence and help us seize every moment as a chance to witness Your life in us. Amen.

THANKSGIVING:

Thank You for the disciples who met You on the road to Emmaus, who questioned and doubted before recognizing You at table. Thank You for restoring their hearts so they boldly told others about Your resurrection. May we join them in gratitude, overflowing with stories of Your mercy. Amen.

PETITION:

Lord, send Your Spirit to live within us today. Open our minds to understand Your ways and our voices to declare Your glory. Strengthen our feet to walk in Your light, where all nations may hear Your good news.

Make us eager servants who live for a world hungry to see Your life. Amen.

Summary:

Here, the Scriptures declare that Christ's ascension did not leave His followers alone-He sends the Holy Spirit to empower and guide them. The resurrection's power must not be kept hidden but proclaimed with joy. We are called to embody this witness, letting His presence transform our lives and point others to Him.

Bible References: Acts 1:1-11 / Ephesians 1:17-23 / Matthew 28:16-20

My own inspiration, thoughts and notes:

WEEK 26 - THE GIFT OF PENTECOST: EMPOWERMENT BY THE HOLY SPIRIT

SHORT PRAYER:

Spirit of God, come and fill us today. Pour out Your gifts freely, knitting our hearts together in one purpose. Let us speak boldly, united in Your name. Amen.

LONG PRAYER

God, I'm trembling like a leaf, half-sure You even hear me - yet here I stand, just another sinner in the stale air of my brokenness. But tonight, I remember Your breath roaring like a wildfire in the upper room, shattering the shutters of the apostles' fear. Don't let my smallness silence me, Spirit - breathe Your power into my lungs right now, and let my mouth speak words that explode with Your life, not mine. Fill me not as a weapon, but as a vessel - messy, cracked, yours.

CONFESSION:

Lord, we confess that we often rely on our own strength instead of Your Spirit. We've ignored the tongues and gifts You've placed within us, treating our lives as self-sufficient. Forgive our hesitancy to welcome Your fire, and burnish our hearts to be vessels of Your power. Amen.

THANKSGIVING:

Thank You, Lord, for sending Your Spirit like wind and flame-dividing tongues but uniting hearts. Thank You for the apostles who stood in awe, for the Samaritan believers who recognized Your might. You're the giver of wisdom, courage, and love; may we bow in gratitude. Amen.

PETITION:

Lord, awaken the gifts You've given us: prophets' clarity, healers' touch, teachers' insight. Fill the gaps of division with Your peace; fill the deserts of despair with Your hope. Make us a church that moves in perfect harmony, as You intended. Amen.

Summary:

Pentecost shows us that God does not choose the weak or powerful- He makes holy a nation through Your Spirit's arrival. The chaos of many tongues becomes a testimony to one mighty God who unites and transforms hearts. We're called to bear this witness: to live as a community where the Holy Spirit is visibly at work.

Bible References: Acts 2:1-11 / 1 Corinthians 12:3b-7, 12-13 / John 20:19-23

My own inspiration, thoughts and notes:

WEEK 27 - GOD'S MERCY: REPENTANCE AND NEW HEART

SHORT PRAYER

Lord, fill me with your relentless love and compassion.

Turn my stony heart into one tender with your grace. Remind me that your mercy always precedes your demands.

Amen.

LONG PRAYER

Lord, take my breathless heart and carve into it your unending mercy.

I stand before you today, a sinner in need of the great I am

who is full of mercy and grace. You do not punish me for-

ever but shower me with forgiveness-not as I deserve, but

as your compassion demands.

CONFESSION:

O Lord, my hands are often calloused by pride, my heart hardened by self-will. I confess I too easily forget the fire of your holiness that parted the sea and still burns across my path. Every offense-big or small-lingers like soot on my soul. Forgive my slow repentance; renew my spirit with the breath of forgiveness. Amen.

THANKSGIVING:

You are love personified, the one who gives us life so we can taste your kindness. You do not force us to love you; you free us to receive your unearned grace. Each morning, my broken heart becomes a vessel for your presence-fragile, yet transformed. Amen.

PETITION:

Change my heart, Lord, as you have promised. Let me walk in your shadow of mercy, bold yet humbled, no longer clinging to the old covenant of fear but dancing in the new one of love. Fill my days with Your glory and shape me into a living reflection of Your faithfulness. Amen.

Summary:

In this season, Scripture whispers of God's mercy-not as empty permission but as the active fire that purges and refines. His commands are not burdens but invitations to trust His relentless love. Every verse here is a mirror: revealing how we fall short yet calling us to lay ourselves at the feet of the One who is mercy.

Bible references: Exodus 34:4b-6, 8-9 / 2 Corinthians 13:11-13 / John 3:16-18

My own inspiration, thoughts and notes:

WEEK 28 - BREAD OF LIFE: SUSTAINED BY THE SPIRIT'S FEAST

SHORT PRAYER

Heavenly Father, feed my soul with your life. Let me hunger only for the bread that never withers. Teach me to receive your gift with open hands. Amen.

LONG PRAYER

Heavenly Provider, let my spirit devour the Bread that is not for passing hunger but for eternal life.

The manna in the desert lasted but one day; yours is eternal. You, Jesus, became flesh for this moment-breaking and bleeding to fill our empty hunger.

CONFESSION:

Lord, I take Your provision for granted. I have tasted Your grace yet still murmur against its abundance. I want the quick fix of worldly strength, not the slow, sacred nourishment that grows in my soul. Forgive me when I hoard my thanks instead of sharing it. Amen.

THANKSGIVING:

How sweet it is to know that Your Word is my daily manna-both life-giving and transforming! You turn fasting into feasting, drought into fullness. Each time I partake of Your sacrifice on the Cross, my heart becomes lighter, my steps more steady. Amen.

PETITION:

Lord, help me to see-to truly see-Jesus in every broken crumb of mercy, every sip of grace, every quiet moment of Your voice. Let my hunger be for You, never for the world's cheap bread. Grant me the faith to receive, the hands to share. Amen.

Summary:

This week's scripture strips away illusions: Your bread alone satisfies, and You alone sustain. Bread here isn't a metaphor but a lived reality-the daily intimacy with Christ who is our Bread from Heaven. Let every mouth and heart break open in awe of what's been given.

Bible references: Deuteronomy 8:2-3, 14b-16a / 1 Corinthians 10:16-17 / John 6:51-58

My own inspiration, thoughts and notes:

WEEK 29 - HARVEST THE HEARTS: SENT WITH HIS LOVE

SHORT PRAYER

Lord, break my willful ways and lead me as you send your apostles. May I step into your world, carrying light with trembling hands. Fill me with the strength of your Spirit, and use me. Amen.

LONG PRAYER

Lord, today I long to be what I cannot be on my own. My heart flutters with the same fear the disciples did, but I yearn to walk alongside the Master as He calls me. You are not asking me to be perfect; you're asking me to be sent-to touch people with a touch marked by Your wounds.

CONFESSION:

I carry my own burdens, Lord, and it's easier to fear rejection than to trust Your love. When I step out, I question whether I'm strong enough, worthy enough. Forgive my pride in self-sufficiency; turn my fear into faith. Amen.

THANKSGIVING:

Thank You for sending the One who is every sacrifice needed. Your heart is bigger than mine-it is overflowing, compassionate, full of yes. To be part of that story? What humility, what grace! Amen.

PETITION:

Father, take my weak hands and place them on the shoulders of those lost, confused, or alone. Give me the words to speak Your name-simple, true, and bold. Let my stammering mirror my unbelief, but never Your power. Use my doubts to draw others closer to You. Amen.

Summary:

The call echoes through history: You are living water. Go and heal. Not to save, not to judge, but to love. These verses unzip the chest of the Church, revealing not priests or heroes but flawed souls called to bring a world the Bread we've tasted-through hands trembling and hearts wide open.

Bible references: Exodus 19:2-6a / Romans 5:6-11 / Matthew 9:36-10:8

My own inspiration, thoughts and notes:

WEEK 30 - SEEDS OF PAIN: THE GRAIN OF WHEAT

SHORT PRAYER

Lord, plant my tears into the earth of Your mercy. Turn my suffering into fruit that others may drink life from. Let even the sharpest thorn remind me that You are with me. Amen.

LONG PRAYER

God of raw truth, I kneel in the dark before Your Word today. It is a knife-sharpening my soul to hold the scars of Jeremiah's cry and the weight of Christ's sacrifice. You are no sugar coater; You are the one who lets the seed die to bear fruit. Teach me how to carry the cross and how to walk in freedom.

CONFESSION:

Lord, how quickly my pain hardens into self-protection. I shrink from the world's judgments when it's easier to believe they're true. Forgive me when my quiet cries echo with bitterness instead of trust. Amen.

THANKSGIVING:

Your pain is holy! You took my weakness-the thorn that pierced Your side-into Yourself. How can I not rejoice that my smallest struggle is cradled in Your wounds? Every shadow has light there. Amen.

PETITION:

Help me to embrace my pain as a seed. Not to throw it in the dirt, but to plant it deep within the soil of Your love. Let every loss become Your harvest. Let my every prayer be a fire and a song-both-as I bring my burden to You with open hands. Amen.

Summary:

Here the sacred and suffering dance-pain is transformed into resurrection. The world screams injustice, but Your Word whispers: My grace is greater. This season of Lent knows: even the blood of seeds must be spilled to give life.

Bible references: Jeremiah 20:10-13 / Romans 5:12-15 / Matthew 10:26-33

My own inspiration, thoughts and notes:

WEEK 31 - DIVINE PROVISION, TRANSFORMATION & DISCERNMENT IN FAITH

SHORT PRAYER

Father, your love is already planted in us, deeper than doubt and deeper than loss. Help us surrender even what seems precious in this world, that we may receive the true life only you give. May every act of faith become an act of love. Amen.

LONG PRAYER

Heavenly Father, every morning I wake to a world that whispers security is found here - in wealth, in control, in the approval of others. But Your Word speaks differently. It says "Do not cling to what is yours, but offer yourself instead." Open my hands like the widow's jar, not to hoard, but to multiply what You give.

CONFESSION:

God, I confess: I've hidden things from You-not to protect others, but myself. Fear keeps me from giving too freely, love from taking risks, and prayer from being utterly yours. When I hesitate in generosity, is it because I trust You more than the promise of security? Teach me to trust this-that the less I hold, the more I'll have. Amen.

THANKSGIVING:

You take our broken offerings and make them flourish. You took bread-so ordinary it was almost wasted-and turned it into life. You called a small woman's coin more precious than a kingdom's wealth. For this, Lord, my heart breaks open-not in sorrow, but in awe. My cupboard is not full, yet You multiply its contents. Thank you for seeing our emptiness as a place to pour in. Amen.

PETITION:

When the world tells me to hoard, Lord, remind me: My life is not my own. If You call me to give up comfort, status, or even peace to follow, help my fear bow before Your wisdom. Let me live with such abundance that others glimpse heaven when they see me. And when my faith feels smaller than the challenges before me, hold me close and say: "The one who gives even a cup of cold water in my name will not lose their reward." I trust You, not my hands. Amen.

Summary:

These verses trace a paradox of faith: trusting God often looks like losing control. The widow's offering shows how generosity born of love becomes life. Paul's baptism imagery echoes this-dying to self to live fully in Christ. Jesus' radical call demands that even family bonds be redefined if needed to obey. The theme? Sacrifice is the birthplace of treasure. God rewrites our losses into blessings, making us his instruments.

Bible references: 2 Kings 4:8-11, 14-16a / Romans 6:3-4, 8-11 / Matthew 10:37-42

My own inspiration, thoughts and notes:

WEEK 32 - HUMILITY, HEALING & THE KINGDOM'S NEARNESS

SHORT PRAYER

Lord, let me see Your kingdom as a child sees a king-on a donkey, not a throne. Heal my pride that it may not block Your nearness. May my life offer a resting place for the weary, even if it costs me. Amen.

LONG PRAYER

Lord, when Zechariah prophesied, he painted a picture so stark: Your Messiah comes not with armies or gold, but riding on a colt. How humbling for the world - how scandalous! Yet here, the broken cities sit under Your mercy, and the peoples do not lift their swords against each other. You disarm before we have a chance to lift them. My heart clenches in terror and awe. How often I ask, "How much must I endure?" instead of "How much must I receive?"

CONFESSION:

Father, I admit: I still long for the kingdom to come in fire and fame, not quiet surrender. I try to "earn" Your approval through self-sufficiency, instead of leaning on the Spirit who already lives in me. When I grow weary of the cross, my pride whispers, "This is too hard." But Your way is not hard-it's human. Forgive my eagerness to bypass humility and take Your love by force. Amen.

THANKSGIVING:

You choose the broken-Zion, the scattered, the weary-to show Your kingdom's arrival. You take what the world discards and call it precious. Thank You for bending the heavens and coming low, that we might be healed, not by our goodness, but by Your grace. Your yoke is gentle, Your burden light, and my heart, though weary, is yours to carry. Amen.

PETITION:

When I struggle to see the kingdom in the everyday, renew my eyes. Let the crying of the wounded world meet Your healing hands through mine. May I, like You, offer mercy instead of justice, compassion instead of judgment. And when pride creeps in, remind me: "You who have done this thing, you have done it for Me." So let my small obedience be a gift- not to myself, but to the kingdom's arrival. Amen.

Summary:

These verses reveal a God who comes closer to heal what divides. Zechariah's vision contrasts earthly kingship with heavenly service: a ruler who brings peace, not swords. Paul's assurance ties the Spirit's presence to freedom from sin's shackles. Jesus invites the burdened to exchange their hard labor for His light yoke. The thread? The kingdom arrives in humility, and our part is to meet it with open hands.

Bible references: Zechariah 9:9-10 / Romans 8:9, 11-13 / Matthew 11:25-30

My own inspiration, thoughts and notes:

WEEK 33 - SEEDS, SCATTERING & THE HARVEST OF OBEDIENCE

SHORT PRAYER

> Lord, I plant nothing by myself-only what You give. Help me scatter my life like seed: faith in the dark, hope in the silence. The harvest is Yours - trust me with the sowing.
>
> Amen.

LONG PRAYER

> Father, You promised in Isaiah that Your word would not return empty - it would bring forth fruit and multiply beyond counting. Like the farmer who scatters grain into the field, I watch my prayers, my obedience, my efforts tossed into the unknown. Does it matter if I see no immediate sprout? Does it matter if the soil looks barren today?

CONFESSION:

Lord, I confess: I check the soil too often, afraid to scatter without seeing fertile ground. I water my faith with calculations: "Will this work? Can I measure the return?" Instead of resting in Your promise that the seed will sprout-in due season. Forgive my fear of letting go, my unwillingness to trust the dark. Teach me that the harvest isn't about my labor, but Your grace. Amen.

THANKSGIVING:

Thank You for taking my barrenness and turning it into fields. Thank You for calling me to sow when I'd rather hoard. Your word doesn't fail-it overflows. Your kingdom doesn't wait-it rises. And the scattered seeds I've called "wasted"-You use them to nourish life. In Your hands, my failures become food. Amen.

PETITION:

Lord, I release my concerns to You. Help me to scatter my faith like dust upon the wind-not with control, but with surrender. Let my prayers be rain, my acts of love seed, my obedience soil. And when I fear the harvest won't come, remind me: "The sower sleeps and rises night and day, and the seed sprouts and grows-he does not know how". But You do. So let me rest, scatter, and trust. Amen.

Summary:

This week's verses speak of seeds and seasons: Isaiah's promise of watering and fruiting mirrors the parable of the sower. Paul's cosmic patience echoes the mystery of growth-laboring in faith, yet knowing the outcome is God's. The lesson? Obedience is sowing; growth is divine. The farmer's part is to throw the seed. The harvest? That's yours, Lord.

Bible references: Isaiah 55:10-11 / Romans 8:18-23 / Matthew 13:1-9

My own inspiration, thoughts and notes:

WEEK 34 - WEEDS, WHEAT & THE SOVEREIGNTY OF GRACE

SHORT PRAYER

Father, you see what I don't-the wheat hidden in my brokenness, the grace in my failure. Help me surrender the separating to You. My work is to scatter light, not to harvest righteousness. Amen.

LONG PRAYER

Lord, in Your mercy, You've planted the good seed in my heart. But the field is already invaded-weeds choke, doubts linger, and my faith feels thinner than the soil. Yet You alone know which grain is Yours. Even when my heart is a patchwork of love and resistance, of hope and fear, You work in me. I don't need to pull the weeds-just to let You separate what is and is not wheat.

CONFESSION:

Father, I admit: I try to be the harvester. I pull at the thorns in my life, thinking my labor will spare You the inconvenience. I confuse my righteousness with Your grace. Forgive me for not seeing that even my "good works" are tangled in my own fears. Help me to stop judging the wheat by its weeds and trust You with the work of separating. Amen.

THANKSGIVING:

Thank You for letting me be just a farmer, not a judge. Thank You for calling me to water the fields, not to sort the grain. Your mercy is not a sieve-it's a fire, and You are the smith. Thank You for the grace You reveal in my failures, the life You grow from the seeds I never thought would rise. Amen.

PETITION:

Lord, when my hands tremble to let go, steady me. When my heart aches at the mess, remind me: You will separate wheat from weeds, not me. Let my life be a field where Your grace scatters like gold dust-unseen to the world, but treasured by You. And when I stumble, let my faith become a lantern to light hidden wheat. Amen.

Summary:

These verses paint a story of hidden wheat and persistent weeds. Jesus' parable reveals the reality of mixed fields; Paul's intercession assures us the Spirit sees the wheat in us. Wisdom's prayer celebrates God's mercy as the force that saves both seed and sinner. The heart of it? We don't harvest righteousness - we trust the harvester.

Bible references: Wisdom 12:13, 16-19 / Romans 8:26-27 / Matthew 13:24-30

My own inspiration, thoughts and notes:

WEEK 35 - THE TREASURE, THE PEARL & THE NET: FINDING VALUE IN SACRIFICE

SHORT PRAYER

Lord, help me let go of what I treasure most-that I may find the pearl that changes everything. May my hands be open to hold Your gift, even if it costs me everything. Amen.

LONG PRAYER

My God, in Your economy, everything matters - but not what I thought. Matthew's parables show that what seems lost (a field, a pearl) is actually found. The fisherman's net pulls out both bad and good, and yet everything becomes a gift when You say so. The widow's mite, the young man's possessions - none of it is neutral. It's either treasure, pearl, or hindrance.

CONFESSION:

Lord, I confess: I've hidden treasures from You-status, stability, even my faith's depth-in exchange for temporary security. I've played the fisherman, but when the haul came in, I sorted and sorted, afraid of what You might call good. Forgive me for treating Your love like a pearl to be guarded, not traded for. Let me let go of all I've taken for myself, that I may know You are my pearl, my field, my net. Amen.

THANKSGIVING:

Thank You for turning my empty hands into harvests, my fears into fields You call mine. Thank You for buying me back with Your blood, for seeing me not as a loss, but as treasure. In Your economy, my failures are seeds, my waste is gold. Thank You for letting me trust You with the separating, the keeping, the selling. Amen.

PETITION:

Lord, when the net is full and the world counts its spoils, remind me: My value is not in what I hold, but in Your hands. When my heart clings, stretch me. When my gaze lingers, draw me deeper. Give me courage to sell what must be sold, to burn what must be burned, and to scatter what must be scattered-for Your kingdom's sake. May I, like the pearl merchant, know no price too high for You. Amen.

Summary:

A week of treasure parables: Matthew's images (fields, pearls, nets) reveal that what looks like loss (a field for sale, a single coin, a full haul of fish) is where the divine meets the human. In Paul's writing, his heart for all is clear-no separation, no wasted labor. The message? The kingdom finds what the world counts valueless and turns it to gold. Our job? To trust the net to hold both good and bad, and to let go.

Bible references: Matthew 13:44-52 / Romans 1:14-22

My own inspiration, thoughts and notes:

WEEK 36 - HOPE IN UNSHAKEN LOVE

SHORT PRAYER

Dear God, when life feels fragmented, You gather us with Your word and promises. Like bread and wine sustained Jesus and His disciples, nurture our hearts with Your grace. Help us trust in Your steadfast love, even when doubt creeps in. Amen.

LONG PRAYER

Father, the scriptures whisper of Your provision - like the feast of free grace in Isaiah, where You call the weary to feast without cost. Today, we stand in awe that even when the winds of hardship howl, Your love is an immovable anchor. Jesus, recall how You drew apart to teach, yet Your heart broke when crowds still sought Him. Help us learn from Your exhaustion, yet trust that Your power and mercy multiply where we need it most.

CONFESSION:

We confess, Lord, when our trust wavers like shifting sand. When we tire of hunger, You feed our souls-will we still seek You, or chase crumbs instead? Forgive our distracted hearts, Lord. Lord, when fear rises like the sea around us, remind us: You are not distant. Grant us to see Your face even in storms, as Peter did. Amen.

THANKSGIVING:

Thank You, Lord, for feeding us with Your Word - more plentiful than five loaves divided. Thank You for declaring, "Nothing can separate us from Your love". Thank You that even as Your followers doubted on the water, Your hand was extended, not condemning, but drawing us deeper into mercy. Amen.

PETITION:

Lord, heal our hunger for control. Teach us to rest in Your provision like bread broken for the many. When we shrink from You or fear Your "deep waters," reveal Yourself anew. Amen.

Summary:

These verses anchor hope in God's unshakable love through hunger, trust, and miraculous provision. Isaiah's call to freely eat is echoed in Jesus' multiplication of bread, while Paul insists divine love conquers all. The disciples' desperate journey and Peter's faithless plunge reveal the paradox: God sustains us even as He calls us beyond our limitations.

Bible References: Isaiah 55:1-3 / Romans 8:35, 37-39 / Matthew 14:13-21

My own inspiration, thoughts and notes:

WEEK 37 - LISTENING FOR DIVINE WHISPERS

SHORT PRAYER

Lord, when the storm howls and I ache for answers, teach me to listen not for storms, but for Your still voice. May I like Elijah hear the silence as Your presence, and like Peter's faith in You amidst waves, lean on Your grace when doubt rises. Amen.

LONG PRAYER

Heavenly Father, the scriptures paint Your presence in unexpected ways-like the wind or fire that Elijah sought but missed in the earthquake or blazing furnace. Yet You, God, speak not in fire, but in the whisper that reveals Your heart. In Romans, Paul pleads with a God whose "glory" exceeds understanding, yet gives "grace" even to His "crucified" one. Jesus, in the chaos of stormy seas, invited Peter to "Come" into the impossible.

CONFESSION:

Lord, forgive when I demand fire instead of faith. When I hear Your voice like thunder, I forget how to quiet my heart enough to hear Your "This is My Son". Forgive my pride in seeking strength before seeking surrender. Help me rest where You place me, even if the "fire" of my passion turns to fear. Amen.

THANKSGIVING:

We thank You, Lord, that You reveal Yourself in the places I seek to bypass-like Elijah fleeing, only to hear the small voice of tenderness. Thank You for a God who does not reject His people but calls us to radical love, though they remain weak. Thank You for the wind of Your Spirit, even when the storm rages in my soul. Amen.

PETITION:

Lord, make me more like the "quiet" in the storm, the "still small voice" I long to recognize. Teach me to hear Your call in ordinary moments, whether as Jesus' name on Peter's tongue or grace breaking through my unbelief. Amen.

Summary:

Here, God's presence is revealed in the absence of fanfare-like the whisper of mercy to Elijah, the silent storm in Peter's heart. Paul's raw sorrow over Israel's hardness is mirrored in Jesus' "stretched out" arms over wavering faith. These verses invite us to find Your voice in the wind and the fire, where faith and fear collide.

Bible References: 1 Kings 19:9a, 11-13a / Romans 9:1-5 / Matthew 14:22-33

My own inspiration, thoughts and notes:

WEEK 38 - WIDENING OUR HEARTS FOR ALL

SHORT PRAYER

Lord, open our eyes to see the "foreigners" among us - like

the Canaanite woman who knelt with persistent faith.

Break down our walls, just as You widened Yours to em-

brace all who seek Your mercy. Amen.

LONG PRAYER

Heavenly Father, Isaiah calls out to a world still building

"gates" of inclusion, while Paul longs for Israel's repent-

ance, yet celebrates the grafted - in Gentiles. Like the

woman who refused to be dismissed, You teach us the cost

of desperate faith - yet You reward those who dare to

trust. In Your hand, Peter's initial rejection of feeding

"pigs" became a lesson in bold love.

CONFESSION:

Lord, we confess our "pigeonholing"-labeling neighbors as "outsiders" when You create hearts to be like Yours. Forgive our doubt when grace seems too vast for those unlike us. Teach us like the woman who cried through "foreignness" to find Your mercy. Amen.

THANKSGIVING:

Thank You for Your promise: "The foreigner and fatherless"-even they will find Your mercy". Thank You for Paul's insight: "Their adoption .. and their riches and glory, all belong to them!". Thank You for the woman who, though mocked, refused to let Your kindness close before her. Amen.

PETITION:

Father, widen our circles like Your feast tables, where no one is unwelcome. Give us the faith to persist in love - even when walls seem impenetrable. Amen.

Summary:

Here, You invite us to expand our "gates" from legalism to love, like Isaiah's invitation to foreigners and Paul's longing for all to taste the "deep mysteries" of Your grace. Even Jesus, who "opened" the heavens to a woman seen as a "dog," shows us that His mercy is unbounded-when we dare to beg or believe.

Bible References: Isaiah 56:1, 6-7 / Romans 11:13-15, 29-32 / Matthew 15:21-28

My own inspiration, thoughts and notes:

WEEK 39 - THE HEART OF SERVANT LEADERSHIP

SHORT PRAYER

> Lord, when we grasp the "keys" of leadership, remind us
> like Shebna and Peter that true service kneels - not at a
> throne, but at the feet of those Jesus served. Teach us to
> yield to You. Amen.

LONG PRAYER

> Father, Isaiah strips Shebna of his title, replacing him with
> Eliakim - "a keyholder" yet one who bears the cross of ser-
> vice. Paul declares Your inexplicable "glory and wisdom",
> while Peter's declaration - "You are the Christ!" - unlocked
> faith's next stage. Here, "keys" become more than author-
> ity - they are tools to bind and loose His mercy.

CONFESSION:

Lord, forgive our envy when others hold "keys" we lust for. We confess: our hearts cling to titles like Shebna's, rather than the cross. Teach
us like Peter - "You are the Christ!" - and drop all but trust. Amen.

THANKSGIVING:

Thank You for Eliakim's rise - a man with no pride but divine purpose.
Thank You, Paul, for celebrating Your "mystery of wisdom" beyond hu-
man calculation. Thank You for Peter, who traded pride for proclamation.
Amen.

PETITION:

Lord, let every leader's hand be softened like keys to a heart's door.
Teach us to "bind" selfishness and "loose" Your grace. Amen.

Summary:

These passages weave authority with humility - from Isaiah's servant-king to Paul's praise for Your "hidden wisdom". Peter's vision in Caesarea echoes here: You turn keys into keys to doors, opening kingdoms to the broken. True leadership is always about kneeling.

Bible References: Isaiah 22:19-23 / Romans 11:33-36 / Matthew 16:13-20

My own inspiration, thoughts and notes:

WEEK 40 - THE CROSSWAY'S CLARITY

SHORT PRAYER

Lord, when the "crossway" confuses our steps, show us like Jesus that the road with nails leads to light. Grant us the courage to "take up our cross" each day. Amen.

LONG PRAYER

Heavenly Father, Jeremiah's prayer is raw: "Cursed be the day I was born!" - yet You turn lament into life. Paul invites us to "present our bodies as living sacrifices", and Jesus: "The cross is the path to life". Here, the voice is clear - "If anyone wants to follow Me!" - but the cross is still the price.

CONFESSION:

Lord, we confess: we'd follow Jesus on a mountain, not a hill of thorns. Forgive our flinching from the "cross" of daily surrender. When we see Christ's glory, help us remember the bruised hands that shaped it. Amen.

THANKSGIVING:

Thank You, Jeremiah, for a "lament that became prophecy." Thank You, Paul, for calling us to "transform" our lives around Your cross. Thank You, Jesus, for teaching Peter "the gates of hell" are no match for the nails of love. Amen.

PETITION:

Father, make the path we walk feel like the "hunger" Jeremiah knew- to only hunger for Your word. Burn off our reluctance when we'd exchange the cross for easy roads. Amen.

Summary:

Here, life's "crossway" becomes the lens: Jeremiah's suffering birthed his mission, Paul's cruciform living redefines worship, and Jesus' own "cross talk" is a declaration-"This is the only way." No detours granted.

Bible References: Jeremiah 20:7-9 / Romans 12:1-2 / Matthew 16:21-27

My own inspiration, thoughts and notes:

WEEK 41 - THE CALL TO WATCHFULNESS AND LOVE

SHORT PRAYER

God, remind me to be a watchful soul, loving like You love-speaking truth in love and acting with tender urgency. Open my ears to warnings and my heart to the lost. Help me carry Your light, unconditionally. Amen.

LONG PRAYER

Lord, the weight of Your call on my life feels both clear and overwhelming - watch over others like You watch over me. Help me guard what is holy in them as if their very souls depended on my wisdom and compassion. Let love be my witness, even in rebuke, for love always bears witness to truth. When my own pride whispers, "They know what they're doing," let me still speak. Remind me that my words have eternal weight, that mercy must outlast my patience. Bind my tongue to mercy and my heart to hope.

CONFESSION:

Forgive me when I assume righteousness in my silence, when I dismiss others as beyond saving. Forgive the bitterness I carry - toward my own failures or their stubborn hearts. Lord, my love often serves itself, and justice becomes a shield against inconvenience. You demand more of me: unconditional watchfulness, like a shepherd checking the flock even when they refuse to listen. Have mercy on my half-hearted obedience. Amen.

THANKSGIVING:

Thank You that love is never passive. How gracious it is that You gave me ears to hear, eyes to see, and arms to guide others back to the fold. Lord, thank You for the privilege of carrying Your truth-when it stings to love and discipline, when it's exhausting to keep holding out Your hand to those who turn away. You are the Love that never gives up on us. Amen.

PETITION:

God, teach me to listen like a prophet. When bitterness lingers, soak it in Your grace. When I fear confrontation, give me courage to speak softly but surely. Bind me to the lost, even when no change seems possible. And Lord, when my heart hardens-whether theirs or mine - thaw it with Your love. Renew my patience like fresh dew, so that love doesn't die from neglect or fear. Amen.

Summary:

This week's words call us to watchfulness, like a shepherd tending the flock. Truth demands love, not division, yet correction is love in action. We're commanded to be the living words that bind or mend broken relationships. Warning is not for judgement - it's an act of desperate care.

Bible references: Ezekiel 33:7-9 / Romans 13:8-10 / Matthew 18:15-20

My own inspiration, thoughts and notes:

WEEK 42 - FORGIVENESS, MERCY, AND THE WEIGHT OF DEBT

SHORT PRAYER

Jesus, teach me the heartbreak of mercy-let my forgiveness be as fierce as Your love, and may I never settle for bitterness. Show me the debtors and my own trespasses in need of pardon. Amen.

LONG PRAYER

Jesus, Your mercy was active - even when people demanded it. You bound yourself to debts no one else would bear, and then asked more of those You loved. This week, help me understand mercy as more than a transaction - it's a rebellion against the chains that bind.

CONFESSION:

Lord, forgive me when I love in proportion to the other person's effort, when I keep a ledger of hurts like a debt I'll never settle. Forgive the hypocrisy of my prayer-Lord, forgive us our debts as we forgive others - spoken as if I were God, not Your servant. You bore the weight of unforgiven sins, and my grudges are but chaff compared to the fire of Your mercy. Amen.

THANKSGIVING:

Thank You for the freedom of relational debt cleared-not by my merit, but by Your command. Thank You for the servants who forgive over and over, even when repentance seems empty. Thank You that mercy isn't earned; it's received as a sacred gift and given as an act of worship. You didn't forgive because we were good; You forgave because You were just in love. Amen.

PETITION:

Show me the debts I haven't paid-both those of others and my own. Teach me to see debtors through Your eyes, like the man forgiven 10,000 talents, not like an insolvent landlord. Burn out the lies: "They'll never change." "I've forgiven enough." Instead, Lord, make my heart as vast as Your mercy, that I might carry the freedom of another's pardon as a balm for my own wounds. Amen.

Summary:

This week's verses remind us that mercy is reciprocal-and never passive. We're called to forgiveness that repeats itself daily, like the Master who pressed his servant to love again. Forgiving others releases us from the prison of debt, even when no repentance seems sincere. Ultimately, it's a love that refuses to be a one-time act-it becomes a way of life.

Bible references: Sirach 27:30-28:7 / Romans 14:7-9 / Matthew 18:21-35

My own inspiration, thoughts and notes:

WEEK 43 - DIVINE JUSTICE AND HUMBLE TRUST

SHORT PRAYER

Father, help me surrender all my expectations of fairness- let my trust rest in You alone. Show me the hidden justice in my life, even when it feels unjust. Amen.

LONG PRAYER

God, justice isn't about being treated right - it's about trusting You in the middle of the not yet. Isaiah's challenge remains: "Seek the Lord while He may be found", even when justice feels slow or absent. Your work isn't for un- derstanding; it's for obedience - like a vine trusting the gardener for the fruit it can't yet see.

CONFESSION:

Forgive me when I love the timing of Your justice more than You. When my patience wears thin, I reduce You to a fairy godparent - here to make me happy or make others pay. Forgive my faith that demands proof be- fore I praise. And when I compare my labor to another's, forgive the pride that whispers: "It isn't fair that I should keep going." Amen.

THANKSGIVING:

Thank You that my reward is Yours to give, not mine to judge. Thank You for the final justice-the day when no labor will feel unjust, when mercy triumphs over timing. And Lord, thank You that my unseen work is counted just the same as the visible. Amen.

PETITION:

Renew my trust in Your will. Teach me to long for the final act of jus- tice-when all the delayed, the wronged, the weary shall have their rest. Keep me from withering in the middle when the harvest isn't mine to see. And when my soul aches for immediate fairness, remind me: "There was no room for me to change the wages" - but You changed my heart to see that mercy is Your work alone. Amen.

Summary:

We're asked to seek You while the world remains unjust-a call to trust in Your power to recreate what's been delayed. The vineyard parable warns against both pride (thinking we deserve more) and despair (dismissing others' value). Your justice is complete - waiting for the day when we'll lay down our partial understanding and step into Your finished one.

Bible references: Isaiah 55:6-9 / Philippians 1:20c-24, 27a / Matthew 20:1-16a

My own inspiration, thoughts and notes:

WEEK 44 - THE REPENTANCE OF A HARDENED HEART

SHORT PRAYER

God, soften my heart before You. Let me see the sin I've tolerated-mine and others'. Help me plant Your word now before hard soil takes root. Amen.

LONG PRAYER

Father, Ezekiel's rebuke still stings: "The sinner will not live by their sin". Even now, I hold onto sins I refuse to name-the habits of the tongue, the slow patience with my own wandering heart, the silent justifications I've built like walls around my life. Yet You still offer the gate.

No one deserves Your call to repentance - least of all me, the one who loves reasons more than restoration. But You will have mercy - even when I prefer the fruit of my labors over the root of Your grace. Jesus, when my heart feels hard as flint, remind me that You seek and save the unwilling more than the willing.

CONFESSION:

Lord, forgive my comfortable sins-the ones I've tolerated for years, the compromises I call "practical." Forgive the doubt I've stored like almond trees that bear no fruit. Forgive my self for becoming the just landlord-"You reap what you sow" - when I've yet to acknowledge my own harvest of sin. Amen.

THANKSGIVING:

Thank You that the sinner is forever invited back-even after the flaws of my heart have hardened. Thank You for the second vine, the new chance for repentance even when my old ways seem embedded. You don't force us to repent-You wait, and wait some more. Amen.

PETITION:

Scatter the flint from my heart, O Lord. Root out the justifications I've made to keep from seeing my true condition. Let my sins ache enough to make me run to Your grace, not away from Your presence. And Lord, when I judge others' choices from my comfortable heights, remind me: "It isn't over until the last leaf breathes". Amen.

Summary:

Ezekiel's words are both a warning and a hope - sin has consequences, but the door is never shut. Your justice doesn't cancel mercy; it calls for it. Even my unwilling repentance becomes Your work - a fruit planted in stubborn soil and then watered into life.

Bible references: Ezekiel 18:25-28 / Philippians 2:1-11 / Matthew 21:28-32

My own inspiration, thoughts and notes:

WEEK 45 - THE COST OF BLIND DISOBEDIENCE

SHORT PRAYER

> God, wake me up from my complacency. Let me see how
> my "safe" choices echo the choices of wickedness in Your
> story. Show me the path of obedience where love and light
> grow. Amen.

LONG PRAYER

> Lord, the vineyard burns - "A man had a vineyard and put it
> under guardians, and went away". Yet what's even more
> chilling is who rejected what was meant for good. The
> housebuilders, the tenants, the shepherds in the same field
> - they all knew. Your warning today is not about ignorance,
> but willful turning away from the fruit You've cultivated.

CONFESSION:

Lord, forgive me for being a tenant who works but refuses to own the land. Forgive the sin of taking without gratitude-my time, my talents, even my pain as my own. Forgive my quiet complacency - calling sacrifice a choice and obedience a restriction. When I feel the burden of repentance, remind me that You didn't send Your Son to demand better, but to give better. Amen.

THANKSGIVING:

Thank You that Your word endures in the midst of rejection. Thank You for the vineyard that still yields - even among those who seem indifferent. Thank You that Your love transplants the heart, not just replaces it. Even the wicked's eventual ruin is a mercy. Amen.

PETITION:

Wash away my unseen idolatry - my love of control over what You call grace. Help me to see the cost of every day - the blood of the Lord of the vineyard that I take as my own. May I never again find comfort in the illusion that I've planted my own obedience. Amen.

Summary:

In these verses, You warn that knowledge of the way leads to account-ability - not just for the sinner, but for the well-meaning blind as well. The vineyard parable is a mirror for our worship: "My house is a house of prayer", but only until it becomes "a house of robbers." The challenge today: let Your light bear fruit, not rot in what we're willing to accept.

Bible references: Isaiah 5:1-7 / Philippians 4:6-9 / Matthew 21:33-43

My own inspiration, thoughts and notes:

WEEK 46 - THE FEAST OF THE LORD: GLADNESS AND ETERNAL CELEBRATION

SHORT PRAYER

Heavenly Father, fill our hearts with the joy of Your feast where every sorrow is turned to laughter and every tear is wiped away. May we, like Your servant Paul, find strength and contentment even in trials, trusting You hold the feast of our redemption in Your hands. Prepare us, Lord, to meet You with open arms, not like careless guests, but as beloved children longing to dance in Your light. Amen.

LONG PRAYER

Oh Lord, our souls long for the celebration that never ends-the feast You prepare where no guest shall be unwelcome. Revelation speaks of a table set for all nations where every tear is wiped and every fear silenced, and we yearn to see this feast in flesh. Yet, Lord, before that day dawns, Your Spirit already gifts us with fragments of that joy: the quiet gladness of faith, the deep contentment born of suffering borne for Your name.

CONFESSION:

We come, Lord, not as worthy servants, but as children whose faith sometimes wavers and whose hearts are heavy with hesitation. Too often, we come unprepared-shallow in our devotion, distracted by cares. Forgive us when we shrink from Your call to holiness, when we trade our robes for the world's clutter, when we forget the privilege of standing before You. Cleanse us from every stain of pride or neglect, that we might be found ready in the end. Amen.

THANKSGIVING:

Yet You, Lord, are faithful! Even now, You feed us with Your Word and nourish us with Your Spirit - preparing us for the greater feast. Paul wrote of finding sufficiency in his poverty and overflowing thanks even when stripped bare, because you, O Lord, are all I need. Thank You for the grace that already makes us partakers: the baptism that baptizes our souls, the communion that binds us to Your body and blood, the hope that stirs our hearts to sing, "Now we see but dimly, yet then face to face." Amen.

PETITION:

Prepare us, oh Lord! Unclothe us of our own wills and arm us with Your Spirit so that when You say, "Come, feast with Me," we stand clothed in Your righteousness, not our own works. And when the lost of this world are cast out in darkness, let us be beacons of Your mercy-the ones who invite the wayward home. Awaken in us a hunger for the feast that never fades, and teach us to love the guests You send, not the gifts they bring. Amen.

Summary:

The readings paint a picture of eternal feasting - God's radical welcome in Revelation, Paul's joy in affliction in Philippians, and Jesus' parable of the banquet where all who enter are dressed for holiness. Together, they challenge us to live as though already at table: ready, repentant, and radiant with the hope of that feast which is our future and our today.

Bible references: Isaiah 25:6-10a / Philippians 4:12-14, 19-20 / Matthew 22:1-14

My own inspiration, thoughts and notes:

WEEK 47 - GOD'S SOVEREIGNTY - WORSHIP THE ONE WHO OPENS WAYS

SHORT PRAYER

Lord, every nation has its kings, but none can move mountains like You. Open our eyes to see Your hand in every turning, every ruler's rise and fall, and bend our wills to worship You alone. May our lives reflect the truth You have set ablaze in our hearts-living not for praise from men, but for Your glory. Amen.

LONG PRAYER

Father God, the prophets proclaim Your rule is absolute-You stretch out the heavens, call the stars by name, and set the kings in place like You command. Isaiah's vision breaks through the lies of idolatry: "I form the light, I create the darkness; I make well-being and create disaster" - nothing escapes Your hand or heart. Yet, Lord, even Your anointed people sometimes stumble, letting pride or fear dim the light of Your sovereignty.

CONFESSION:

How we forget, O Lord! How easily we bow to lesser gods-wealth, fame, the idol of control - and call it "wisdom" or "patience." We praise Your power in abstract but shrink from offering it to others, like the Pharisees who tested Jesus about taxes, not to seek justice, but to trap Him into betraying Your truth. Forgive us when our obedience is performative, when our prayers seek our own ends, when we trade Your glory for comfort. Strip away our hidden motives, Lord. Renew our hearts to love You without reservation. Amen.

THANKSGIVING:

But You, Lord, have done what we could not - You broke the hardened soil of our hearts and planted Your Word there. The Thessalonians' story is ours too: Your Spirit took root in the midst of trials, producing a people whose love overflowed even amid persecution. You call, and they believed! Thank You for the fire of truth You kindle - that it burns in our bones and lights our lips to sing Your name without shame. Thank You that no earthly authority can silence Your Spirit or outshine Your light. Amen.

PETITION:

Lord, today we surrender our nations, our lives, and even our silences to Your kingship. Uncover the "idols" we honor in secret - the resentment, the greed, the fear of what could be ours. And when others try to put You on trial or bind You to their systems, let our words ring with Your voice: "Render to Caesar what is Caesar's, but to God what is God's." Root us in Your sovereignty over all, that we might rise and love as You love-without calculation, without end. Amen.

Summary:
Isaiah decree is clear: God uses rulers as His instruments, yet He calls all nations to bow. Thessalonians models hearts ignited by the Word, undaunted by trial, while Jesus' reply to the Pharisees exposes the hollowness of motives without the light of His love. We are called to witness to the One who is the Way - the One nations must bow before.

Bible references: Isaiah 45:1, 4-6 / 1 Thessalonians 1:1-5b / Matthew 22:15-21

My own inspiration, thoughts and notes:

WEEK 48 - THE CALL TO JUSTICE AND LOVE OF NEIGHBOR AS YOURSELF

SHORT PRAYER

Father, guide us to love as You command-justly and deeply, with mercy for all. Open our eyes to see the oppressed as You see them, and fill our hearts with Your tender compassion. Help us walk in Your paths of righteousness with joyful obedience. Amen.

LONG PRAYER

Lord, as we gather before You, we remember Your laws etched in stone and written upon the tablets of our hearts. The words of Exodus urge us to care for the vulnerable and the foreigner, to lift up the downtrodden and defend the widow and orphan. Let these commandments echo in our minds and stir our souls to live with justice and mercy - not as duties but as love.

CONFESSION:

Lord, I confess that I often prioritize my ease over Your call to love. I've failed to see the widows, the orphans, the strangers around me as You do. I've harden my heart to plead for justice, or to open my hands to give. Forgive my apathy, my greed, and my fear of sacrifice. Today, I surrender all-to Your justice, Your mercy, and Your perfect love. Amen.

THANKSGIVING:

Oh, what a miracle it is, God, to serve You by loving others. Thank You that in You, love is not just a word - it's a way of life. Thank You for the church that mirrors Your heart, for the hands that feed the hungry, the voices that cry out for the oppressed. Thank You that Your justice is not cruel but redeeming. Amen.

PETITION:

Lord, open my eyes to the needs around me. Fill me with boldness to love with Your love-not just those who deserve it, but all. Help me listen to the forgotten, stand with the weak, and welcome the outcast. Give me a heart that burns with Your justice and compassion, even when it costs. And when love feels impossible, remind me that You are faithful. Amen.

Summary:

These passages call us to a righteous life rooted in justice and love. Exodus teaches us to protect the vulnerable and the stranger in our midst. Paul reminds us that love is the fulfillment of the law, urging us to walk in righteousness, not just for obligation, but for the transformation of our hearts. Jesus ties these truths together: love God and love your neighbor are the greatest commandments, and in them, we find freedom and fullness of life.

Bible References: Exodus 22:20-26 / 1 Thessalonians 1:5c-10 / Matthew 22:34-40

My own inspiration, thoughts and notes:

WEEK 49 - THE BLESSED AND HOPE OF HEAVEN'S SHELTER

SHORT PRAYER

Holy Spirit, draw me close to the shelter of Your wings.
May my heart rest in the promise of eternity, where suffer-
ing ends and hope finds its home. Keep me steadfast in
Your truth and peace. Amen.

LONG PRAYER

God of mercy, today I bow before You, knowing that in
Your presence is fullness of peace. Revelation speaks of the
shelter of Your throne, where the earth's weary find rest
from war and sorrow. You, who call us blessed, promise a
refuge beyond our understanding - a place where all is
made new. Let this hope anchor my soul, that no storm
may overwhelm me.

CONFESSION:

Father, I confess my unbelief. I've forgotten that heaven is my eternal home, and my present struggles are but a brief moment. I've worried more about tomorrow than trusted in Your promises. I've missed the blessing in waiting, choosing instead to dwell on what feels urgent rather than what is eternal. Forgive my myopia, my fear of the unknown, and my reluctance to live as one who longs for heaven. Turn my eyes upward, Lord. Amen.

THANKSGIVING:

Your Word is full of hope, Lord. You've promised a throne, a shelter, and a people who've overcome because You are faithful. Thank You that in the midst of life's battles, You've always prepared a place for me. Thank You that no matter what I face today, my name is written in the Lamb's book of life. Thank You that Your grace is bigger than any storm. Amen.

PETITION:

Lord, let my heart ache less for what's temporary and more for what's eternal. Help me to live with Your peace, speak Your hope, and trust in Your timing. When fear creeps in, remind me that You are already victorious. Grant me a soul that thirsts for heaven, a life that seeks Your glory above all. And when I'm weary of waiting, stir my hope once more. Amen.

Summary:

These verses paint a picture of heaven - a safe, triumphant refuge where God's people are secure, washed in His grace. The first John's letters speak of new life in Christ, calling us to rise above the brokenness of the world. The Beatitudes reveal that blessing is found in humility and righteousness, even in suffering. Together, they remind us that our hope is not fleeting but rooted in God's unshakable love.

Bible References: Revelation 7:2-4, 9-14 / 1 John 3:1-3 / Matthew 5:1-12a

My own inspiration, thoughts and notes:

WEEK 50 - THE PREPARATION FOR ETERNITY: VIGILANCE AND REWARD

SHORT PRAYER

Jesus, keep my lamp filled with Your light, that I may be ready to greet You in Your glory. Grant me wisdom to use my time well, and faith to trust in Your return. Amen.

LONG PRAYER

Lord of all time, Your Word speaks of judgments and rewards - of doors that shut, lamps that go out, and the surprises of the future. But in this, You teach me to live with purpose, ready for the day when my work will be tested. Help me see this life as a preparation, where every moment matters in the grand story of Your kingdom.

CONFESSION:

Father, I confess my half-heartedness. I've lived for comfort instead of faith, for convenience instead of obedience, and often, I've missed the urgency of Your call. Forgive my slumbering spirit, my fear of the unknown, and my tendency to forget that my life's work is for Your kingdom, not my own gain. Turn my eyes back to Your return, my heart to service, and my strength to action. Amen.

THANKSGIVING:

Your Word reminds me, Lord, that You are coming again - to reward the faithful and call the righteous home. Thank You for the grace that makes preparation possible. Thank You that You are not one to sleep but to wake at Your appointed time. Thank You for the church that stands firm, for the souls who are faithful, and for the hope that fuels every step. Amen.

PETITION:

Lord, pour out Your vigilance in me. Help me to live with purpose, ready to meet You at any hour. Give me the courage to share Your light, the wisdom to walk in truth, and the patience to trust in Your timing.

When fear rises or my faith wavers, remind me that I belong to You. Keep me steadfast, lovingly prepared, and eager for Your return. Amen.

Summary:

These passages call us to live with purpose and watchfulness. Wisdom urges us to seek God's light and justice, emphasizing the consequences of our choices. Paul's letter teaches that death is not an end but a transition, calling believers to live with the hope of resurrection and final reward. The parable of the ten bridesmaids warns of readiness-our lives must align with Christ's return, lest we miss the gates of heaven. Together, they remind us to live intentionally, trusting in God's grace and justice.

Bible References: Wisdom 6:12-16 / 1 Thessalonians 4:13-18 / Matthew 25:1-13

My own inspiration, thoughts and notes:

WEEK 51 - THE LEGACY OF WISDOM AND STEWARDSHIP

SHORT PRAYER

God, guide my steps to reflect Your kindness and wisdom.

Help me to invest in lives and tasks with Your love. Teach

me to see each day as an opportunity to serve and honor

You. Amen.

LONG PRAYER

Father of wisdom, Proverbs and Matthew teach us to

honor diligence, generosity, and love - not just in words but

in action. Today, I seek Your help to walk in these virtues.

Fill me with strength to build with purpose, to share with

grace, and to live with the stewardship You intend for my

life.

CONFESSION:

Lord, I confess my selfishness. I've hoarded Your gifts when they were meant to bless others. I've feared failure more than I've trusted in You. Forgive my resistance to Your call to serve, my tendency to judge others' efforts, and my lack of generosity in spirit. Help me to live as one who builds with joy, who shares with no strings attached, and who trusts in Your perfect timing. Amen.

THANKSGIVING:

Your Word, Lord, is full of examples of good stewardship-the strong woman who gives bread to the poor daily, the master who entrusts talent and expects fruit. Thank You for the grace to follow Your lead, for the strength to act when called, and for the rewards of a life lived in obedience. Thank You that Your blessings are meant to bless others. Amen.

PETITION:

Lord, fill me with Your wisdom. Give me a heart to invest in people, resources, and opportunities as You intend. Help me to act with courage, to trust in Your provisions, and to live as though every day could be my last. May my life be a light, a legacy, and a reflection of Your love for the world. Amen.

Summary:

The proverbs celebrate a woman who lives with excellence, generosity, and industry. Paul calls the church to vigilance and wisdom in serving others, and Jesus warns of how we steward our gifts. These passages remind us that a meaningful life is not measured in comfort but in how we honor God with our hands, hearts, and resources.

Bible References: Proverbs 31:10-13, 19-20, 30-31 / 1 Thessalonians 5:1-6 / Matthew 25:14-15, 19-21

My own inspiration, thoughts and notes:

WEEK 52 - THE SHEPHERD'S PROMISE AND THE LAST JUDGMENT

SHORT PRAYER

Lord, today I trust in Your care as the Good Shepherd. May Your voice guide me, and may my heart reflect Your compassion toward all creation. Grant me the courage to serve, not for my glory, but for Yours. Amen.

LONG PRAYER

Lord of all, Ezekiel's vision of the shepherding Spirit fills me with hope - promising restoration, healing, and divine intervention in the lives of those scattered. Yet this is also the week of judgment and final reckoning, where every hidden and unveiled thing will be made plain. Draw me into Your presence, Lord, that I may see with Your eyes and live with Your justice.

CONFESSION:

Father, I confess my hardness - I've seen suffering and ignored it, judged others harshly, and missed opportunities to bring healing. I've trusted my own strength rather than Your voice, my judgment instead of Your mercy. Forgive my fear, my pride, and my blindness to Your call. Turn my heart toward Your flock, and grant me the courage to tend them as You do. Amen.

THANKSGIVING:

You are the Great Shepherd, Lord, and Your promises are sure. Thank You for the prophetic word that declares restoration, for the hope that You will gather all things in Christ. Thank You that Your justice will be met with mercy, and Your reign with salvation. Thank You for the joy of knowing You will judge rightly-and heal completely. Amen.

PETITION:

Lord, make me a voice for Your compassion, a hand for Your justice, and a heart that echoes Your voice. Help me to love with Your love, to serve with Your courage, and to trust in Your timing. When fear rises or the world seems broken, remind me that You hold all things together. Give me a spirit of boldness and gentleness, that my life may proclaim Your kingdom. Amen.

Summary:

Ezekiel's vision comforts the hurting and promises restoration, while Paul and Jesus speak of our call to serve with love and justice. Ezekiel reminds us that our Shepherd's care is all - encompassing - saving, healing, and gathering. Paul assures us that Christ will judge with mercy and justice, separating the just from the unjust. Together, they call us to live with the tenderness of a shepherd and the boldness of a prophet.

Bible References: Ezekiel 34 / 1 Corinthians 3:10-15 / Matthew 25:31-46

My own inspiration, thoughts and notes:

USED CHRISTIAN YEAR CALENDAR WITH ALL BIBLE REFERENCES

In total 52 weeks according the liturgical calendar topics starting with the 1st week of Advent:

1: Bible reference: Is 2:1-5/Rom 13:11-14/Mt 24:37-44

2: Bible reference: Is 11:1-10/Rom 15:4-9/Mt 3:1-12

3: Bible reference: Is 35:1-6a, 10/Jas 5:7-10/Mt 11:2-11

4: Bible reference: Is 7:10-14/Rom 1:1-7/Mt 1:18-24

5: Bible reference: Sir 3:2-6, 12-14/Col 3:12-21 or 3:12-17/Mt 2:13-15, 19-23

6: Bible reference: Is 60:1-6/Eph 3:2-3a, 5-6/Mt 2:1-12

7: Bible reference: Is 42:1-4, 6-7/Acts 10:34-38/Mt 3:13-17

8: Bible reference: Is 49:3, 5-6/1 Cor 1:1-3/Jn 1:29-34

9: Bible reference: Is 8:23—9:3/1 Cor 1:10-13, 17/Mt 4:12-23 or 4:12-17

10: Bible reference: Zep 2:3; 3:12-13/1 Cor 1:26-31/Mt 5:1-12a

11: Bible reference: Is 58:7-10/1 Cor 2:1-5/Mt 5:13-16

12: Bible reference: Sir 15:15-20/1 Cor 2:6-10/Mt 5:17-37 or 5:20-22a, 27-28, 33-34a, 37

13: Bible reference: Gn 2:7-9; 3:1-7/Rom 5:12-19 or 5:12, 17-19/Mt 4:1-11

14: Bible reference: Gn 12:1-4a/2 Tm 1:8b-10/Mt 17:1-9 (25)

15: Bible reference: Ex 17:3-7/Rom 5:1-2, 5-8/Jn 4:5-42 or 4:5-15, 19b-26, 39a, 40-42

16: Bible reference: 1 Sm 16:1b, 6-7, 10-13a/Eph 5:8-14/Jn 9:1-41, 6-9, 13-17, 34-38

17: Bible reference: Ez 37:12-14/Rom 8:8-11/Jn 11:1-45 or 11:3-7, 17, 20-27, 33b-45

18: Bible reference: Mt 21:1-11 /Is 50:4-7/Phil 2:6-11/Mt 26:14—27:66 or 27:11-54

19: Bible reference: Acts 10:34a, 37-43/Col 3:1-4 or 1 Cor 5:6b-8/Jn 20:1-9 (42) or Mt 28:1-10 (41) or, Lk 24:13-35

20: Bible reference: Acts 2:42-47/1 Pt 1:3-9/Jn 20:19-31

21: Bible reference: Acts 2:14, 22-33/1 Pt 1:17-21/Lk 24:13-35

22: Bible reference: Acts 2:14a, 36-41/1 Pt 2:20b-25/Jn 10:1-10

23: Bible reference: Acts 6:1-7/1 Pt 2:4-9/Jn 14:1-12

24: Bible reference: Acts 8:5-8, 14-17/1 Pt 3:15-18/Jn 14:15-21

25: Bible reference: Acts 1:1-11/Eph 1:17-23/Mt 28:16-20

26: Bible reference: Acts 2:1-11/1 Cor 12:3b-7, 12-13/Jn 20:19-23

27: Bible reference: Ex 34:4b-6, 8-9/2 Cor 13:11-13/Jn 3:16-18

28: Bible reference: Dt 8:2-3, 14b-16a/1 Cor 10:16-17/Jn 6:51-58

29: Bible reference: Ex 19:2-6a/Rom 5:6-11/Mt 9:36—10:8

30: Bible reference: Jer 20:10-13/Rom 5:12-15/Mt 10:26-33

31: Bible reference: 2 Kgs 4:8-11, 14-16a/Rom 6:3-4, 8-11/Mt 10:37-42

32: Bible reference: Zec 9:9-10/Rom 8:9, 11-13/Mt 11:25-30

33: Bible reference: Is 55:10-11/Rom 8:18-23/Mt 13:1-23 or 13:1-9

34: Bible reference: Wis 12:13, 16-19/Rom 8:26-27/Mt 13:24-43 or 13:24-30

35: Bible reference: 1 Kgs 3:5, 7-12/Rom 8:28-30/Mt 13:44-52 or 13:44-46

36: Bible reference: Is 55:1-3/Rom 8:35, 37-39/Mt 14:13-21

37: Bible reference: 1 Kgs 19:9a, 11-13a/Rom 9:1-5/Mt 14:22-33

38: Bible reference: Is 56:1, 6-7/Rom 11:13-15, 29-32/Mt 15:21-28

39: Bible reference: Is 22:19-23/Rom 11:33-36/Mt 16:13-20

40: Bible reference: Jer 20:7-9/Rom 12:1-2/Mt 16:21-27

41: Bible reference: Ez 33:7-9/Rom 13:8-10/Mt 18:15-20

42: Bible reference: Sir 27:30—28:7/Rom 14:7-9/Mt 18:21-35

43: Bible reference: Is 55:6-9/Phil 1:20c-24, 27a/Mt 20:1-16a

44: Bible reference: Ez 18:25-28/Phil 2:1-11 or 2:1-5/Mt 21:28-32

45: Bible reference: Is 5:1-7/Phil 4:6-9/Mt 21:33-43

46: Bible reference: Is 25:6-10a/Phil 4:12-14, 19-20/Mt 22:1-14 or 22:1-10

47: Bible reference: Is 45:1, 4-6/1 Thes 1:1-5b/Mt 22:15-21

48: Bible reference: Ex 22:20-26/1 Thes 1:5c-10/Mt 22:34-40

49: Bible reference: Rv 7:2-4, 9-14/1 Jn 3:1-3/Mt 5:1-12a

50: Bible reference: Wis 6:12-16/1 Thes 4:13-18 or 4:13-14/Mt 25:1-13

51: Bible reference: Prv 31:10-13, 19-20, 30-31/1 Thes 5:1-6/Mt 25:14-30 or 25:14-15, 19-21

52: Bible reference: Ez 34:11-12, 15-17/1 Cor 15:20-26, 28/Mt 25:31-46

ABBREVIATIONS OF THE BIBLE BOOKS

Old Testament:

Amos Am	Exodus Ex	Jeremiah Jer
1 Kings 1 Kgs	Nahum Na	2 Samuel 2 Sm
Baruch Bar	Ezekiel Ez	Job Jb
2 Kings 2 Kgs	Nehemiah Neh	Sirach Sir
1 Chronicles 1 Chr	Ezra Ezr	Joel Jl
Lamentations Lam	Numbers Nm	Song of Songs Sg
2 Chronicles 2 Chr	Genesis Gn	Jonah Jon
Leviticus Lv	Obadiah Ob	Tobit Tb
Daniel Dn	Habakkuk Hb	Joshua Jos
1 Maccabees 1 Mc	Proverbs Prv	Wisdom Wis
Deuteronomy Dt	Haggai Hg	Judges Jgs
2 Maccabees 2 Mc	Psalm(s) Ps(s)	Zechariah Zec
Ecclesiastes Eccl	Hosea Hos	Judith Jdt
Malachi Mal	Ruth Ru	Zephaniah Zep
Esther Est	Isaiah Is 1	
Micah Mi	Samuel 1 Sm	

New Testament:

Acts of the Apostles Acts	Philemon Phlm	1 John 1 Jn
Mark Mk	Galatians Gal	2 Thessalonians 2 Thes
Colossians Col	Philippians Phil	2 John 2 Jn
Matthew Mt	Hebrews Heb	1 Timothy 1 Tm
1 Corinthians 1 Cor	Revelation Rv	3 John 3 Jn
1 Peter 1 Pt	James Jas	2 Timothy 2 Tm
2 Corinthians 2 Cor	Romans Rom	Jude Jude
2 Peter 2 Pt	John (Gospel) Jn	Titus Ti
Ephesians Eph	1 Thessalonians 1 Thes	Luke Lk

The Latin Names for Days of the Week:

The days of the week in Latin are named after planets and gods, using the structure "dies [Planet/God's Name]": **dies Solis** (Sunday, day of the Sun), **dies Lunae** (Monday, day of the Moon), **dies Martis** (Tuesday, day of Mars), **dies Mercurii** (Wednesday, day of Mercury), **dies Iovis** (Thursday, day of Jupiter), **dies Veneris** (Friday, day of Venus), and **dies Saturni** (Saturday, day of Saturn).

These names directly influenced the Romance languages (like French, Spanish) and even Germanic languages (English).

WHY BIBLE AND BOOK STUDY GROUPS ARE A MUST

BREATHING LIFE INTO SCRIPTURE

Why Reading Together is More Than Just Reading:
   Scripture says, "Iron sharpens iron, and one friend sharpens another" (Proverbs 27:17). There's no faster way to deepen your walk with God - or discover the hidden truths in stories - than sitting in a room (or Zoom call) with people who're just as hungry for wisdom as you are. But what does a Bible/book study group actually offer? How does reading together - really reading, with messy questions, honest doubts, and shared tears transform lives?

Whether you're a seasoned reader of sacred texts or just starting, study groups unlock three things we rarely get on our own:
   Community, clarity, and courage. Without them, the risks of misreading, spiritual stagnation, or even complacency loom. This post breaks down five core benefits of joining a study group (backed by scriptural wisdom, psychology, and real-life examples) and closes by naming the hidden dangers of doing spiritual growth solo.

So pour a cup of coffee (or tea – no judgment), grab a highlighter and a notebook, and let's explore how groups help us do theology - not just talk about it.

1. THE POWER OF SHARED MEANING:

Reading Together Demystifies the Bible.
   "The word of God is living and active" (Hebrews 4:12). But the problem? The Bible doesn't come with a built-in translator.
   What sounds poetic in one context ("God is love," 1 John 4:8) might leave others frozen by fear of misinterpreting it to mean they have to earn God's affection. Reading in a group exposes that ambiguity—and clarifies it.

Why it works:
   Context is everything: When a verse like Revelation 13's "beast" comes up, your pastor or group might link it to Rome, tyranny, or even modern systems of oppression. That discussion? It turns a cryptic symbol into a lived reality.
   Avoiding "spiritual bypassing": Without a group, we're tempted to gloss over hard questions (e.g., "Why does God seem slow to act?"). But in a group, peers ask, "What's in it for me?" and "How do I see hope in this?" – forcing us to wrestle before we "claim" a verse.
   Scripture takes shape: A poem like Psalm 23 feels like a cliché until

someone shares how they're wrestling with grief or God's silence. Suddenly, "even though I walk through the valley" hits different.

Example: After reading the crucifixion story in Mark, one group spent three sessions debating: Was Judas a scapegoat? Was Jesus the victim, or the one who chose the path? A solo reader might default to comfort ("Jesus always wins."). But in a group, someone asks, "What if the greatest lesson is that grace starts in the struggle?" – a shift that changes how you read Jesus' prayer from Gethsemane.

Picture the scene: You're holding a well-worn Bible at 7 AM, while your group leader – over coffee – suddenly leans forward and says, "I didn't get this until I read 1 Corinthians 13 on grief – my mom died. The verse 'love does not insist on its own way' broke me open. It wasn't about perfect love... it was about God's love when I insisted." The group quietens. Even non-churchgoers nod in recognition.

2. CHARACTER GROWTH THROUGH ACCOUNTABILITY (BECAUSE NO ONE NAILS IT ALONE)

"We confess our sins to one another..." (James 5:16). Confession often implies accountability – but what gets held accountable?

In solo reading, our ego gets to call the shots: "I know the Bible says sin is forgiven, but my life proves God's slow to act." But in a group, a sister who's been in recovery might challenge: "That's called shaming your sorrow, not seeing your need for grace." And suddenly, the Scriptures actually start to form in you.

Why it works:

Nakedness meets grace: In Psalm 51, King David's confession is raw – "Against you, you alone, have I sinned." But without a group to witness, we're less likely to say that our pride hides behind actual sins. Study groups force vulnerability, because no one believes, "I'll never need this again."

The "why" gets clearer: You struggle to pray but know the Bible says prayer changes things. In a group, someone else admits they've abandoned prayer for years, and someone else says, "For me, it started when I realized God wasn't asking for perfect words – he wanted me in the mess." The "why" wasn't about rules; it was about people like you.

Spiritual maturity isn't a race: A group leader might say: "I've memorized whole chapters of Revelation, but it took losing a job to see what 'faith' meant. My 'wisdom' didn't help me. What's yours holding back from God?"

Scripture moment: John 14:26 says the Holy Spirit "teaches you everything and reminds you of what I've said." But what if the Spirit's promptings need a "roommate" to amplify them? Groups serve as that roommate - pointing out what your eyes skip over or your spirit deflates.

Risk to avoid: Groupthink! (We'll get to that.)

3. INTELLECTUAL GAINS: THE BIBLE IS A THICKET WITHOUT GUIDES

"Seek to understand before you're understood." (Romans 12:9) Reading the Bible alone is like hiking the Grand Canyon by yourself — you don't even know the cliffs are dangerous until you fall off. Study groups bring:

Disciplinary rigor: Did you read Genesis 1 as a scientific text? Did you read Job as philosophy? Groups show you how to parse narrative (exodus story), letter (Paul's epistles), law, and poetry.

Historical and cultural context: Reading Daniel's lions' den without knowing "kings and satraps" where Persia's hierarchy might leave you thinking it's about animal attacks. A group clarifies: It's about a world literally running by fear. Now it feels like a personal warning.

Facing cognitive dissonance: You think love is a choice — but Paul writes to slaves that "servants obey your earthly masters" (Ephesians 6:5). A group helps you unpack: "How does love also mean submission?" There's no one right answer. Just the honesty to wrestle.

Psychological insight: Studies show reading together increases retention. One 2018 research paper (Journal of Bible Translation) found that group discussions improve comprehension by up to 22% because people process content through others' eyes.

Try this: Bring a favorite passage you've read a hundred times. Read it aloud, then ask: "Why does this story feel like a mirror? What's the hard part in this verse for me?"

4. EMOTIONAL HEALING THROUGH SHARED SUFFERING

"Come to me, all who are weary and burdened" (Matthew 11:28). Reading scripture without a community? It's like having a first-aid kit but never using the Band-Aids. Groups offer:

A safe space for "dark nights": In a group, a member might say, "I read Romans 6 and thought God wanted me 'dead to sin' — so I stopped eating. Now I hate it." Others share how to read it as union, not punishment.

Story-sharing as healing: Psalm 6:7 says, "Lord, my soul suffers pain." A group doesn't just read this — someone says, "Me too." Suddenly, loneliness about grief or betrayal or rage isn't just intellectual; it's an actual wound that Scripture can tend.

Countering false promises: A pastor might preach, "God won't let bad things happen to believers." In a group, someone's spouse died of can-cer: "What is my verse to God? 'All things work for good'? When you're drowning?"

Key Bible lesson: In Isaiah 53, the prophet describes Christ's suffering *"like a lamb to the slaughter" – not a triumphant war cry. Groups help readers understand why Jesus chooses to walk through the valley, rather than bypass it.

5. DEEPER FAITH THROUGH DIVERSE LENSES

"No eye has seen, no ear has heard .. the things God has prepared for those who love Him" (1 Corinthians 2:9).

Perspective shift: A retired mission worker might interpret Ephesians' "prison" verses as "freedom in the Lord," while a homeless member says they've felt trapped there. Suddenly, both sit with an expanded faith.

Generational wisdom: A grandma might say, "In my day, Psalm 137's 'hang my harp on the willow' was a lament – but today we think it's about resilience. Was she sick of her exile?" Now a young member reads it as personal mourning, and national suffering.

The world outside the church: A study group once read Romans 13:1-5 (loyalty to authority) and included a single mom in an abusive relation-ship: "My Bible says obey your ruler .. but I need safety." A lawyer who read it as a business leader was forced to say, "I didn't see it's the same text – so where is its love?"

THE RISKS OF READING ALONE (BECAUSE EVEN GOOD THINGS HAVE SHADOWS). NO TOOL IS NEUTRAL. STUDY GROUPS ARE BLESSINGS – BUT THEY'VE BLIND SPOTS:

Groupthink: "Everyone says I'm wrong for not loving my neighbor." (E.g., seeing only Jesus' grace in John 8's "let him who is without sin cast the first stone".) Risk: You stop trusting your own conscience.

Fear of standing out: A group's leader reads Ezekiel's valley of dry bones as a metaphor for revival...but you're mourning a child. Risk: Si-lence – "I can't ask why my grief doesn't sound 'hopeful.'"

The "group's agenda: "Some groups preach "justification by faith alone" as if all other interpretations are wrong. Risk: You lose your voice.

Superficial unity: A pastor reads "God provides" (Matthew 6:25–34), and the group laughs when someone "tests" their "faith" on a budget. Risk: You miss the verse's critique of hunger for more – and your own hoarding.

Dependence without independence: A group member never learns to study on their own, and one crisis makes them panic: "I never figured out Hebrews 12 alone!" Risk: It becomes a crutch, not a lifeline.

How to navigate: Before joining a group, pick one: "I need a group where

I'm allowed to ask 'Why does God do X?' – even if my pastor never does."

HOW TO START YOUR OWN GROUP (EVEN IF YOU'RE A NEWCOMER)

You don't need credentials. Just:

Find a theme: Start with Psalms (for emotion), John's gospel (for grace), or Paul's letters (for justice).

Pick a rhythm: Weekly Zoom chats, a monthly book study, or a 12-week course.

Invite questions: "Bring a question you have about the verse – not what the 'answer' is."

No prep required: Bring a coffee or sandwich. Study groups aren't seminars - they're meals where people talk about your faith, not about being "spiritual enough."

Final scripture: Matthew 18:20 says, "Where two or three are gathered in my name .. there I am with you." Not for grand theological debates – with you. In the confusion. In the tears. In the laughter as you try to understand "love your enemies."

WHERE TO GO FROM HERE

Try a small step: Pick one chapter to discuss with friends. Ask: "If God wanted us to know 'X' in this story, what's not getting said?"

Join a pre-made group: Online platforms like Bible Gateway (free) or Goodreads have book/discussion lists.

Remember: Your "slow start" at reading or praying is the point where most people find out how small God's love is for them.

CLOSING QUESTION

What's one verse or story you've re-read a million times - only to suddenly see it in a new way after sitting with other believers?

 **Get discounted Author copies as a Group Book Order:**

ABOUT THE AUTHOR

Born into an Italian carpenter heritage family, Christian Crafts brings a rich cultural background and a deep appreciation for the natural world.

He grew up in the rhythm of hands-on craftsmanship, which has influenced his storytelling and attention to detail.

A devoted Christian, that finds inspiration in faith and community, often weaving those themes into his work.

Married with children, a military veteran who served with honor and dedication, grounding him in resilience and responsibility.

Holding an engineering degree, that blends technical precision with creative narrative, crafting stories that explore the intersection of human ingenuity and the beauty of nature.

Passionate about the outdoors, loves hiking, camping, and connecting with the earth, which often finds its way into the settings, characters and challenges of his books.

THANK YOU FOR READING - REVIEW

Thank you for reading.
If you enjoyed this book, I would be incredibly grateful if you could leave a quick review on Amazon.

Thank you and may God bless you all.

 **Amazon KDP Review**:

 If you like to write me direct your comments, you can **get in contact with me by email:**
books@christiancrafts.us

 **Get a FREE ePUB or PDF copy** of this book. Direct download from ChristianCrafts.us Website:

www.ingramcontent.com/pod-product-compliance
Lightning Source LLC
Chambersburg PA
CBHW010934120626
46552CB00010B/3256